I0615729

The Nothing

Also by Lauren Davis

When I Drowned
Home Beneath the Church

The Nothing

Stories

Lauren Davis

YESYES BOOKS

The Nothing © 2025 by Lauren Davis

Cover art: "#4042-B" © Todd Hido

Cover & interior design: Olivia M. Hammerman
Lead project editor: KMA Sullivan
Author photograph: Maegan Gray

ISBN: 978-1-946303-05-9

Published by YesYes Books
YesYesBooks.com

KMA Sullivan, Publisher
Karah Kemmerly, Managing Editor
Devin Devine, Assistant Editor
Olivia M. Hammerman, Graphic Designer
Jill Kolongowski, Manuscript Copy Editor
Gale Marie Thompson, Senior Editor
James Sullivan, Assistant Editor

for my beloved Charlie

Contents

Into the Sun

We awake and the sun is on us and our arms are not around each other. There's a field. The high grass is dry, dying. My hands are earth-stained. The wind—absent. The land lacks cattle, gnats, birdsong.

Where are we? he asks, though his lips do not move.

My hand is over my eyes. I spot a wire fence in the distance, and beyond it, a hedge of leafless trees. The fence curves around the horizon—north, east, south. To the west of us, there's a slight hill. The sky is empty.

How did we get here? he asks, though his mouth doesn't open.

It is unexceptional, this countryside. My palms are on the ground. I am trying to steady myself.

Jonathan, I say.

What? he says. When he speaks, his voice echoes.

There is no sound.

Before we woke here, Jonathan had been on the Pacific Crest Trail. I had asked to join him, but he told me he needed to do it alone. He talked about growing into himself, wanting to fully become the man he was destined to be so that he could do right by me. I'd told him he was everything. My protests didn't matter.

I have to, he had said.

At least let me go with you, I had said.

You cannot know what it means to love you, he'd said, and he pulled me into his arms and his hands were warm and swallowed my waist and I grew soft and sleepy and he kissed the crown of my head.

The night before he left, his mother texted me.

I don't like this, she wrote.

I don't like this, either, I wrote back.

I stayed by the phone, tried to distract myself with work and writing and the TV. He had just proposed a few months ago, at sunset on a mountain. The ring silver, blue-stoned, too large for my finger, but I put a bit of tape around the band. I rubbed the ring like a rosary.

He'd trained for a couple of weeks, going on long climbs in the morning and the evening. His gear looked professional, expensive. Brand new.

We stretch our legs, our arms. We wander toward the fence. But when we are within a few feet of it, we cannot near it. We are no closer to it, no matter how much we walk. The land seems to stretch and contract, like water finding shape. Or a rubber band, a snake that coils, strikes.

Jonathan narrows his eyes. He tries to run at the fence. He gains a few feet, and then the fence moves away from us. Or we move away from it.

Are we on drugs? he says.

I'm not on drugs. Are you on drugs? I say.

No. Are we asleep? he says.

I don't know, I say. *Try to wake up.*

How do I do that? he says. *Come here. Hold my mouth shut.*

Seriously? I say.

Just do it, he says.

He sucks in air, and I place my palm over his lips. The seconds slow, and then he struggles away from me, wheezing.

We need to wake up, he says. He gasps for breath.

Should we try the other direction? I say.

He puts his palm on the small of my back.

Yes, he says.

This time the horizon allows us to come closer to it, and the hill reveals its slight incline, dotted with white flowers and dandelions.

I've failed you, he says.

What do you mean? I say.

The whole point of that hike was to make sure I knew how to be strong for you. Now we're stuck in whatever this is.

I'm tired, I say.

We fall back asleep in the weeds, though I do not dream.

The sun won't set here. When we wake, we're hot to the touch.

We travel about a mile until we spot a cliff. Beyond it—nothing but sky. The cliff reaches as far as we can see, from east to west. In both directions, the fence meets the edge.

Where do we go now? I say.

We build a bridge, he says.

There's no other side to build to, I say.

Of course he knows this. I try to say it kindly.

He steps toward the edge, and the edge moves away from him. He sits, puts his hands over his face. He stays still for a long time. I turn from him and face the fence. I sprint at it. The fence moves away from me. I creep toward it. It creeps away.

He says, *Remember that first weekend I slept over? We stayed in bed, ate ice cream. Your cat wasn't sure about me. In the morning when I woke up, he was sitting on my chest, watching me.*

I kiss his forehead.

We could just jump off the cliff and see what happens, he says, his smile strained.

It won't let us, I say.

What if we close our eyes? he says.

Maybe another day, I say.

There are no days here, he says.

Why do you think we're here? he asks.

I'm not sure if he expects an answer. I don't give him one.

Maybe it's my fault, he says.

What do you mean? I say.

I did something, maybe, he says.

What could you have possibly done? I say.

I don't know. I was on the trail. It had been three days. You know this. Then I went into the trees to change my clothes. They'd gotten damp. They were uncomfortable. I left my pack next to the trail. I was trying to be decent.

He sighs, rubs his eyes.

I looked up and an elk was staring at me, he says. *It frightened me, it was so huge. When it turned and left, I finally relaxed. I hadn't realized I had stopped breathing. I tried to find the trail again. I guess I got turned around, got lost. The forest was so dense, and my compass wouldn't work. I didn't know the trees could swallow you like that.*

I'm here, too, though, I say. *I'm stuck here with you.*

Then what happened? he says.

I had been lying on the couch, writing a story in my notebook. I had set the scene. A field. A fence. A cliff. Then the phone rang. When I answered, the policewoman told me another hiker had spotted an orange backpack in the woods. Inside was Jonathan's ID. The hiker yelled for him, and waited, but he never appeared.

Have you heard from Jonathan? the policewoman said.

He called me two days ago, I said. *But not since.*

We are opening a missing person's report on him, she said.

I would love to see a pigeon. Just a single spider. Or a small, pathetic cloud. To feel a breeze. To have the choice, if I desired, to plummet.

Help me dig, he says.

Dig what? I say.

We can try to dig ourselves out of here, he says.

We only have our hands, I say.

The soil is soft. Help me, he says.

The first layer is powdery. Then there is grit, which cuts into our skin. Our knuckles turn red, bloody. Then we feel a hard surface, unforgiving. I try to ignore the pain in my fingers. I throw handfuls of dirt over my shoulder.

What is that? Rock? Jonathan says.

I spit into the hole, wash off the dirt, see the thick glass. It has a gentle arch, like a large fishbowl.

Help me, I say.

We look down together, our heads touching.

I see myself beneath us. I am lying on my couch. My eyes are closed. Across my chest is an open notebook. The pen has fallen to the floor.

Wake up, I say to the body of me that sleeps. I pound on the glass.

What is this? Is that really you? Jonathan says.

I ignore him.

Wake up, I say again.

I look peaceful there. My cat walks through the room. Overhead, the sun stays steady in her place. The earth does not move.

The One Who
Tucks You in at Night

The elm tree outside my window cut up the moon. I stared at the ceiling, my hand over my heart. I tried to make it beat slow, slower. I would be the master of it. It would answer to me.

Then Monia called. She said, *Come over and sleep beside me. Better yet, let me come over there.*

I said, *What's wrong?*

She said, *There's something in this house.*

And I asked, *What do you mean, like a rodent?*

And she said, *I'm on my way.*

I said that was fine by me, I'd turn the porch light on.

A half hour later, I heard her let herself in. She padded down the hall wheezing and sniffling and banging about. My bedroom door cracked open. Her silhouette seemed delicate. She climbed into bed beside me, and I put an arm over her.

What happened? I asked.

There's something in the house, she said.

Go to sleep. We'll check it out tomorrow.

She took off her socks, held her toes to my shins, yawned, buried her face in my breasts. We were the best of friends.

I'd avoided that house for years.

Then I met Monia. Monia of the scuffed shoes and gnawed nails. Always pale. Her hair like a black river. For her I crawled into the dark.

We met at Adult Children of Alcoholics in a church basement. I had just turned thirty and had started working at a call center downtown.

Everyone had already taken their seats in the metal chairs. The place reeked of drugstore perfume. There was a drone of nose blowing, thin laughter. I'd been going for weeks but had not found my footing. Something about God. I needed a God as I understood that God. But I was not partial to what I could not see.

Monia was standing by a table of cookies, watching the clock. Her blue dress was rumpled.

My name's Carol, I said to her.

Hi, Carol.

I shifted my weight from heel to toe, waiting. She just looked at me.

I said, *And your name is?*

She laughed. *I'm sorry,* she said. *I'm out of practice when it comes to talking to people.*

Don't eat the cookies, I said.

Why? she said.

I brought them. They don't have any eggs or milk. They're disgusting.

No milk? she asked.

Yeah, I said. *They have bran in them, too.*

She gave me a half-smile.

We spent the meeting whispering, giggling, while the guest speaker talked about losing her son. It was grotesque, how we acted, but I think it'd been a while since either one of us had relaxed around another person. What is healing anyhow, if you have to deny joy?

We never went back.

From that moment, we clung to each other like hound's-tongue. Then she moved into my childhood home.

I'd tried to talk her out of it when she'd told me the address a few weeks back.

Have you signed the lease yet? I said to her then.

No, she said.

Why do you need a house that big? I said.

It's dirt cheap, she said.

I think we can find somewhere less weird for you.

What do you mean? she asked.

I mean that's the house I grew up in.

For real? she said.

For real, I said.

That's actually kind of cool, she said.

No, I said. *It's not. It's a bizarre house. We can find you somewhere else.*

I'm definitely renting it now, she said.

My mouth twisted into a grimace.

It's what I can afford, she said. *Why are you acting like this?*

I became quiet. She looked at me curiously, then gathered me in her arms. She had that strange spark people get when they begin to open to their lives after a deep sleep. She'd recently gotten divorced, was working as a shoe salesperson. She had started wearing lipstick and drinking decaf. But she wore a thick layer of heartache on her, too. You could smell it—wet like moss.

The morning after she heard the noise, we stood on her wooden deck—which had at one time been my deck, the place where as a child I'd counted ants, peeled back paint. Monia and I did not speak. I tucked a strand of hair behind her ear. We were the same height, but she always seemed to curve her spine when she was near me so that I hovered over her. She laid her head on my shoulder. Her breathing was shallow, deliberate, like she'd forgotten how to do it properly.

The house, a one-story with a finished attic, had recently been painted an angry red. It was a modest structure at the end of a lengthy gravel road. My mother's peonies were long gone. The stone pathway to the porch had been replaced with concrete, and many trees had been felled. It looked bare without the deep shadows cast by dogwoods. I can't remember who bought the place from my parents, but I knew it had passed through a half-dozen hands. People didn't stick around to grow old there.

Let's get this over and done with, I said.

The kitchen, unchanged, featured an olive-green refrigerator. It smelled, still, like my father's instant coffee. Down the hall, the two windows in the master bedroom opened to an overgrown vegetable garden, then a stand of pines. There were no neighbors within a mile.

Monia had hung heavy brown curtains throughout the whole place to block out morning light. It gave the air a dusty texture. Furnishings were sparse. A solitary recliner, one beige loveseat, one wooden table with two wooden chairs. Every footstep resounded. The ceiling fans had been ripped out, the holes unfilled.

We climbed the worn oak stairs. Monia had put her twin bed in my old room, the attic. She had a velvet comforter, one naked pillow. In a way, her decision to sleep there felt like a compliment. It also troubled me.

When she showed me where the sound came from, my body went rigid. I'd almost convinced myself that perhaps, when she'd first complained of the noise, that it was in fact a faucet or a pipe making racket. Or, worst-case scenario, a trapped sparrow.

The small door in my old bedroom was two feet tall, two feet wide. It was a drabber white than the wall.

That's where I heard it, she said. *There's something in there.*

Probably air pressure, I said.

I chewed my lip, dug my nails under the frame and pried the door open. The hinges sounded as if they were choked with sand. Immediately the room felt changed. Denser. Stonier.

Go in there, she said. She wrung her hands, stared at the opening.

Seriously? I said.

Monia had never looked more like a child. She might as well have been me as a girl, begging my mother to find the monster in the wall. Back then, my mother had inched her slight body inside. When she had crawled out, she had not been the same. That was not the first time I'd seen a change in my mother.

...

Tell me about your parents, I had said to Monia months ago. She was visiting me for the first time. She stood a moment with drink in hand, moving her eyes over my space. I had done everything I could to make my condo look unlike the home I grew up in. I decorated with abstract paintings. All my books on the shelf were hardcovers. My family photos stayed tucked out of sight.

She sat on my couch, rested her chin on her knees.

Oh my God, they were the worst, she said. *Dad would come and he'd have blood all over him from a bar fight and my mother couldn't even greet him she was so drunk. She'd get dinner halfway done. Leave the burner on. I'd finish it up and put the food on the table and I'd have a wet washcloth by the door for Dad. Dad and I would eat in silence while she was passed out in the bathroom.* Monia cocked her head to the side. *It's hard not to feel a little cheated*, she said.

You were cheated, I said.

Yeah, she said.

Let me cook you dinner, I said.

She got really still then, like I'd spooked her.

You don't have to do that, she said.

I know I don't, I said. *What do you like?*

She thought for a moment, but I could tell she was just stalling. *You know what I'd really love?* she said.

What's that? I said.

Will you make me a grilled cheese? she said.

She ate the grilled cheese on the couch with two hands. We watched reruns and then we ate ice cream and then we fell asleep on opposite sides of the couch. When I woke up in the middle of the night, she was mumbling in her sleep. I covered her with a blanket. Without thinking, I kissed her lips.

One late evening, right after she rented the house, Monia and I walked beside Mud Lake right outside a tiny town called Sloan. We came across a fire ring. The park was empty, soundless.

Let's have a bonfire, she said.

Everything's damp, I said. *We should be getting back to the car, anyhow.*

Maybe, she said.

She picked up a few sticks, threw them back. The way she moved in that slender dark, she looked wrong, wild. She got like that sometimes. Had moods. I could nearly taste it in the air.

There was this time my father was out of town, she said. *It was just me and my mom. She got ahold of a bottle of gin. She was mean that night. Yelling. Called me names.* Monia stared out over the lake. *I was having a terrible night already*, she said. *I had just gotten my first period. I wanted to ask questions. I was scared. When my mom passed out with a cigarette in her fingers, I didn't put it out. I wanted to see what would happen.*

Monia stripped off her thin sweater and dropped it in the ring.

What are you doing? I said.

She pulled a lighter from her jeans, bent down, and lit her sweater on fire. She rubbed her naked shoulders and watched.

Do you think we'll always be friends? she said, not looking at me.

Yes, I said.

Then come here, she said.

We should be going, I said.

Look at how it eats away at the neck, she said.

I crouched beside her. The fabric was slow to burn.

As a child, I dreamed I had a sister. Her skin was smooth where a face should have been. We walked in the black of the dreamscape. I grabbed her arm, told her not to go ahead of me. She shrugged me off. I heard a sucking sound, then there was gristle in my mouth. When I woke up, the window was unlocked, the curtains pulled back like hair.

Go in, Monia said, knowing that I would not deny her.

I got flat on the floor. The space was thick with dark.

Do you at least have a flashlight? I asked.

No, she said. *Your eyes will adjust.*

Okay, I said, and entered. I knew the thing was still inside. I could tell by the scent. Sharp. Gamy.

My family had bought the house when I was six years old. My father's boss sent over a fruit basket filled out with bananas.

My mother, first thing, planted tulips. They had never owned a home, and it showed in the extravagant way they danced through the rooms. They tracked in mud. Relaxed into what was theirs. Ordinarily, before my father got up, my mother donned a housedress decorated with angry parrots. She laid out the cereal and opened windows to let in the smell of dew-soaked soil. My father, when he woke up, was always slow to get out of the house and to the quarry.

I think my parents were happy then. They held hands. They chuckled along with the television. We even talked about getting a dog.

I will always remember my family and seven-year-old me and that last night in the Rockies. It was our first vacation since moving to town. My father had rented a log cabin with a large fireplace and a bright green lawn. We'd spent the week catching trout and cheating at cards.

Through the blinds, I watched my father take my mother by the hand and lead her out onto the grass. He dipped her and she laughed, showing all of her throat. They slow danced beneath a haze. She kissed him, and he kissed back.

Then my father left her standing there, and when he came inside and saw me at the window, he smiled.

Is she coming? I asked.

She just wanted a moment to say thank you to the mountains, he said.

I nodded my head, as if I knew what that meant.

He walked off. Down the hall, a light went on. I listened to him get ready for bed—the noise of the sink, a rustle of his suitcase.

Outside the window, my mother had gotten down on all fours. In the wet murk, her back looked hunched. Something seemed to shift beside her, something with weight and grace. The clouds shrugged apart. Her mouth was on it.

The snake turned to look at me, and my mother turned to look at me. I recoiled from the glass, curled my knees to my chest. My father's bedroom light went out.

...

Our house was not the same after that trip. The knocking started. It came from behind the small door in my room, which, up to that point, I had not bothered to explore because the door did not give easily.

I crept out of bed and tiptoed downstairs to wake my father.

The house is talking, I said.

What? he said, groggy, his mouth slack.

Talking, it's talking, I said.

He must have thought I had heard intruders because he grabbed a gun from the dresser.

Upstairs, he sat with me on the edge of my bed and listened.

That's just the radiator, he said.

What's a radiator? I asked.

It's just part of the house, he said.

Which would have made me feel better, if I had believed him. But he just kept sitting there.

You know what, sport? Why don't you sleep in our room just this once? It's important to get good rest, he said.

He clutched my hand as we descended the wooden stairs, and when he turned back midflight to look over his shoulder, I knew he had just told me lies.

My mother, a few days later, snuck beneath my sheets. She was blitzed, blubbering. She smelled like earth and whiskey.

What are you doing, Mom? I asked.

I came to keep you safe, she said.

She grabbed my arms, tugged them around her so that I was forced to hold her limp body.

I could hear my father outside, calling her name.

My mother giggled. *Don't tell him I'm here*, she said. She put her fingers in her mouth to muffle her laugh. *Don't tell. I'll keep you safe, my Carol. Clever Carol.*

I never slept right again. If my father had moved us out early on, we could have been a different family. The longer we stayed, the weaker we became—our eyes glassy, our minds incapable. My mother gave herself over to drink.

One time, when the sound woke me up, I felt rage, a smack of indignation. I hammered on the tiny door with my tiny fists. Then there was silence. Satisfied, I returned to my bed, but I heard something like laughter as soon as I tucked the covers under my chin. After that night, it began a new game. It hummed, and if I did not hum back, it sang, and if I did not sing, it grew loud, so that my hands were over my ears, and I cowered in my sheets, and it laughed.

Shortly after, I was dreaming that dream of my faceless sister. I chewed the inside of my cheek. A hand was over my face, and my body held tight. The house tilted on its side, and through my sleep I could hear my mother scream and my father yell and then he ran up the stairs and shook me awake and gathered me in his arms. He told my mother to follow him, and he rushed us out into the dark and into the car. He drove to the nearest motel, a ten room joint off the highway. He muttered to himself the whole way there.

While he went inside the dimly lit office to pay for a room, we shivered in the car.

Are you okay? my mother said, looking out at the lot, where only a minivan and a small truck were parked.

Yes, I said.

Good, she said.

Mom? I said.

Yes, my dear?

But I did not know how to ask the question, or what the question was.

My mother turned to me, slowly, like it took effort for her to move. Her eyes were two white spheres and she smiled and her smile was a black hole, or so it seemed. I started to cry.

My father returned then with a brass key clutched in his hand. He said, *Come on girls. We'll stay here.*

I did not move. I watched, from the corner of my vision, my mother getting out, stretching.

My father opened my car door, unbuckled my seatbelt, crouched beside me.

It's okay, sport, he said. *We're together.*

My mother and I each slept on opposite sides of my father in the king-sized bed. I could not see her body. I closed my eyes to the sounds of the motel, which were unremarkable and graciously human.

My parents put the house on the market after that, and it sold within weeks.

It was as if my father grew a couple of inches overnight, though with time he began to fold over himself again. My mother never stopped staring at shadows. I don't think my father ever forgave himself. Before their hair turned fully gray, I buried them both.

His heart, the doctor said.

Her heart, the doctor said.

Monia once asked me who I was. *Who are you?* she said. Just like that.

Monia, from the Greek word *monos*—alone, singular, one. She was a little drunk.

I had turned off the movie, turned on my lamp. I heard the neighbor above me clunking around. Monia watched me, and I laughed, faintly.

What do you mean? I said.

She wasn't smiling. She said, *When I'm not here, when no one is here and the TV and the radio are off, who are you?*

It felt, at that moment, like the walls were moving.

I'm Carol, your friend, I said. *The one who tucks you in at night.* I meant for it to sound light, like a joke, but my throat felt thick.

No, she said. *When I'm not here, who are you?*

Something changed behind her eyes. Or, perhaps, I was simply tired, and I saw nothing.

This is weird, I said. I picked up her wine glass, walked into the kitchen. I heard my front door open, close.

I was inside the dark space. I had a metallic taste in my mouth.

What do you see? Monia asked.

Nothing, I said.

Go further, she said.

I pulled my body into the black. I heard something laugh.

I'm coming out, I said. I tried to move backwards, but my arms felt caught.

Not yet, she said.

I stilled my breathing. My body demanded I continue. I felt a heat from something unseen, then I saw light, and I turned my face away.

Look back at it, Monia said. *Open your eyes so I can see it.*

I did as she asked, and she looked through my eyes, and she saw it.

It's beautiful, she said.

I want to close my eyes, I said.

No, she said.

I started to cry. My palms and knees were wet. I smelled the damp, the rot, the years of dark and secret. Doglike, I whimpered.

Closer, she said. *I need a better view.*

Something jabbed at my legs, sharp as a broomstick.

Further, she said.

I pulled myself by my elbows toward it. When I reached for it, it was not myself that reached. It took my hand, which was not my hand. I sobbed, and shook, and tried to move away, but it held me there, and told me things.

I heard Monia from a far distance.

Magnificent, it is magnificent, she said. *Thank you.*

Gone, Ralph, Gone

He wants me. He told me he did. He drives by each evening at 6:00 PM. The officer said old guys tend to stick to routines. Ralph is proof.

There is nothing to be done. Depending on the season, it'll still be light out or it'll be dusk and his hatchback will cruise by real slow and his head will turn toward my closed blinds. He doesn't know I watch for him from the dark upstairs bedroom. Or maybe he does.

David hates it, hates him, hates a lot of things but really hates feeling powerless. Wants to move me in but it's not that simple. There's my lease and this isn't new and I'm not in danger. At least that's what I tell myself. Old guys and their routines. There's no need for Ralph to escalate anything because look how easy and predictable it's all become. I know to start dinner by his slow crawl outside.

When he doesn't show, Wednesday, April, the year of our Lord 2016, I don't open the can of soup. I find myself tapping the wall.

I have not left for the bathroom or shifted focus to my phone. I have waited, as always, at my black window. Until my neck aches and my stomach is a loud hurt.

David calls. Wants to know why I am late. *Flu*, I say. *A rotten one. The worst one.* I hang up.

It is my first day without Ralph.

Walking to my car, I am weak-kneed. When I pull out of the drive, the sweetest song is on the radio. I can't make out all the words, but it's something like, *Look at the moon, it watches you*.

This is a small town. I hit all the major subdivisions in an hour. First down one Holly Acres, then one Jade Valley View. Up Deerwood.

I watch for Ralph's hatchback. There are dozens of streetlamps glowing like small moons. I pay mightily in taxes for this sort of thing.

Drowned Rock is half an hour over, almost but not quite on the way to the ghost town of Sloan. Ralph could be a citizen of some separate city. I had never even considered it.

The miles to Drowned Rock open to patchy fields. The streetlamps stopped miles ago, and the night is fat with clouds. My radio's acting up. Can't catch anything out here. Except the sound of my own mind. How it tells me to drive on.

The Bright

He is a stranger here, opening his strange bakery in a town where fresh bread is an extravagance. But it smells like mothers, like winter after a rain. He turns the corner, and I see him in the frail morning light. I stare, ask him his name.

Andy, he says. It is a simple name, and its simplicity is a lie.

Are you the one that opened the bakery? I ask.

Yes, he says. *And my front bulb just fizzled. Excuse me. I'm on my way to get a replacement. It's too dark in there. Please come in and say hi sometime.*

There is also the fact of his green eyes. His unkempt hair. His tweed jacket over his relaxed shoulders.

Come in and say hi. Come and say hi. He does not know what he has done with those words.

Moses is not a town that can afford luxuries—daily loaves made in an oven, thrown into a dumpster after 3:00 AM if it has not passed hands. I am telling the ghost about Andy, as I tell the ghost about everything, and though I cannot see the ghost or hear the ghost I know the ghost agrees. Imprudent. Real ridiculous.

I don't have enough money. My disability check is meager. But I will eat bread, no matter the cost, because there is a memory in the smell.

I do not go back to see Andy today. I have other things to do—bathe in milk, bathe in salts, write to my dead brother.

I was not always allergic to the sun. Then my family burned in the fire. All light now hurts me. I live in dusk, in layers. The town of Moses greets me in the dawn, and then I am back to my home, drawing the blinds. Each evening I swallow one Plaquenil pill with milk. I think it bleaches my hair, but who knows. The doctor wants me to try phototherapy, though I refuse. He does not push it, because he knows what has happened to me, or he knows the story the rest of the town knows.

I sit down with the ghost to play chess. Sometimes the ghost is slow with its choices. I reach over and move its rook. My king is vulnerable. I move it to the right and fake a yawn. The ghost calls my bluff. Checkmate.

In the morning I dress in a wide brim hat and sunglasses, in a long sleeve tee. I count my dollars and then recount them. The peninsula's sun is sluggish these fall mornings.

I am Andy's first customer. I know this because I stand across the street until he unlocks the door, flips over the open sign on the door's slim window.

He smiles, says, *Hello*. Then I take off my sunglasses and he says, *You. I remember you. Welcome. What can I do you for?* His teeth are stained. His fingers look tender. I watch him clean his small red counter with a rag. He does not have an accent, at least one I can place.

Where are you from? I ask. As soon as I say it, I realize my tone is urgent, not casual, not friendly the way I mean to be.

His hand pauses.

Orcas Island. Born and raised, he says.

I visited once. That place is beautiful. Why would you ever leave?

I look at the loaves, lined up behind bowed glass. They sit on red and white checkered tissue paper. He's put out two of each type, has limited himself to three recipes—wheat, white, and pumpernickel. I admire this restraint.

Why would I ever stay? He laughs. *I was just ready for something new.*

A bell behind me rings. The door opens, a woman walks in. She is not wrapped in many layers like me. I see the top of her cleavage. I feel an odd resentment. Her ears sparkle with yellow jewels, and she smells of jasmine.

Hi Andy, she says, walking past me. *I'll take the pumpernickel.*

He smiles like he knows a secret. After she pays and leaves, his secret smile leaves.

So what can I do you for? he asks me again.

Pumpernickel, I say. I hate pumpernickel. Even the word catches in my throat.

I walk out with the loaf in the crook of my arm, as if it's a baby. The bell chimes when I exit, and the weak sun hits my cheeks. I walk across the road and turn once more toward the bakery. It's petite, the width of an alleyway. It sits between the boarded-up movie theatre and the town's one Mexican restaurant. There's no real sign yet. Andy, or someone, has handwritten the words *Sunrise Breads* on a piece of poster board, taped it to the window.

The way the light strikes the glass, I can't see inside, which means I don't know if he's watching me. I spin to leave, but before I do, I wave, the morning light stinging my hand.

At home the ghost is restless. It wants a name.

Two years. Two years and now you want a name? I ask. Then I realize the unkindness in my voice. *Yes, I will give you a name. What kind of name do you want?*

Silence, and then more silence.

I look over the titles of my books, seeking inspiration. It's been a while since I've read. My neighbors, George and Monique, let me borrow their cable. I turn the TV on and lie down, pat the sofa so the ghost will sit beside me. A newsman talks about mortgage prices, or at least I think that's the story. His tie is too skinny. I have a hard time concentrating.

The ghost is unhappy with me.

I am taking you seriously, I say. *I just don't know yet. Give me a moment. Let my brain relax.*

Then there's a show about making your own pasta, then another about undersea dives.

I turn off the TV and look to the ghost. *How about Ash?* I say. And Ash likes it. And the rest of the evening we play *Scrabble*. Ash wins some, but I win more. It's unusual for me, but I refrain from gloating. At 11:00 AM I turn into bed, letting the sun peak and fall without me.

In my monthly bath of milk, I am Cleopatra. The wallpaper in the bathroom does not flake, does not smell of rot. The lightbulb above the chipped sink is not bare. The cracking linoleum is marble. Honey and rose sit in the air.

I never dilute the milk. It is pure and heavy on my skin. Expensive, but necessary. The cashiers at the corner store no longer bat an eye when I clean out their tidy rows of jugs.

I lie in white and chat with Ash. I recite the story of Patty the Milkmaid, who goes along with a pail of milk balanced on her crown, considering what to buy, wondering aloud. I like to think she has her own ghost she tells these things to. She'll get some fowls from Farmer Brown. Which will lay eggs, which will be sold to the parson's wife. With the money, Patty dreams of buying a new frock and hat. Young men will speak to her at the market. Polly Shaw, whoever that is, will be jealous. Patty, flush in her new fashions, shall toss her head. And as she shows this hair toss to her ghost, the milk balanced on her crown tumbles. She now has nothing with which to entice the young men to speak to her.

I splash my bath. *I no longer like this tale*, I say to Ash. *We need a new tale.*

I see that Ash agrees.

Maybe I should start reading again, I say. *Find something else.*

A hint of light finds its way between the blackout curtains. I suck in a big breath, shut my eyes, lower my face beneath the milk. Parting my lips, I drink.

Brother,

I think sometimes I will live life fully, with a heart filled with love, and that will be the only way I can even begin to make amends. And then I think,

*no, that is the opposite of what I am meant to
do. I am meant to suffer. So it is one of these two
options. I'm really not sure which one is right.*

Love,
Skye

When I buy a white loaf and pass Andy the money, my fingers
brush his. I am thrown by this touch and I fumble the change,
coins clanking. A penny rolls off, and I watch it travel on its slender
rim clear under the countertop. Andy is saying something. He is
smiling. I stutter an apology, scoop up the warm little loaf, leave
half the money laying there.

I am home before I realize that his touch is the first touch I
have felt in nearly two years.

I wait three weeks before I return to Sunrise Breads. Still, in
those weeks, I circle the block many times, catching glimpses of
Andy readying the shop each morning. He is always early. At each
3:00 AM, I note the first sliver of bright behind his counter.

It is a Thursday, 6:00 AM, when I open his door, the bell making
a too-loud chime.

Hello again, he says.

Hello, I say. Clear my throat.

Can I interest you in some bread? He's in a plaid button-down.
Behind him, his tweed jacket hangs on a hook. I wonder if the
smell of yeast clings to the lining, if he carries it into his home,
his bedroom.

Yes, please.

He takes two short steps toward the skinny bakery case, then his hand hesitates on the sliding glass door.

You know my name. What's yours? he asks.

Skye.

That's my daughter's name, he says.

It is? I say.

No, he says. *Sorry.*

We both stare at each other. I click my tongue behind my teeth.

How about a loaf on the house, huh? he says. *It's a Thursday, and Thursday is my favorite day.*

No one has ever offered me a free thing without wanting another thing. *I can pay,* I say.

No, no. White, you like white, right? Don't pretend to like pumpernickel.

I laugh, and he laughs, too.

Skye, tell me. Where are you from?

Here, sort of. We lived further out in the woods. My family and me.

You live here with your family? he asks.

No. I twist in place, drum my fingers against my thigh. *The sun is rising,* I say.

Excuse me? he says.

I have to go, I say.

Here is your loaf.

And he asks no more questions, and I offer no more answers.

Ash, I call out when I return to my cold house. *You won't believe it. He asked about me. Asked me questions.*

I slice the bread, spread the last of the butter on a piece.

Ash, I holler. *Get in here. Are you listening?*

I put down my plate. Everything feels very still.

Not funny, I say. *Where are you?* I move through the tight space, all six hundred square feet. One bedroom, one bath. *Fine*, I say, turning on the TV. I devour the bread as if I am underfed. I leave no crumbs on my plate, sliding a licked finger across my mother's old plates. It is not until I set up the *Scrabble* board that Ash returns.

Seriously, poppycock. *That's an amazing word*, I say, laughing, slapping my knee. *Got me again, Ash. My turn.*

I revisit Sunrise Breads on a Thursday, because it is Andy's favorite day. Now it is my favorite day.

Skye, he says, when the brass bell chimes.

Andy, I say.

How have you been? he asks.

It is a simple question, would be a simple question, if I did not spend each night telling Ash about Andy, about his touch. I've brushed my hair. I spin a black umbrella, though outside there will be no rain. My sunglasses rest in the deep pocket of my long sleeve dress.

I say, *I'm good. How are you?*

Excellent, he says.

We have run out of things to say to one another. When he hands me the loaf, I feel the warmth of his fingers. Briefly. I leave with free bread so fresh it yields a little to my touch.

Brother,

I am writing again to tell you I am sorry. And I am sorry for feeling anything but grief. Sometimes all

I experience is heat. All I smell is melting plastic.
I hear only sirens. But today I felt something like
hope, and I am sorry. Please forgive me. I never
meant to feel anything but fault for the things I
have done, have not done, the thing I did not do.

Love,
Skye

Before I dress for the bakery, I dance unclothed through my rooms to music only Ash and I hear. In the full-length mirror, propped against the wall beside my mattress, I see my body pale and chrysanthemum-bright. I see now that I am beautiful, and I wonder how long I have been beautiful.

Then the secret melody stops, and I freeze. I cannot be a beautiful thing.

It is Thursday, and today, I will do without bread. I am dirty, frayed, so I run a salt bath, create a small scorching sea.

At 8:30 PM, I hear the doorbell. It takes me a second to recognize the sound. I turn on the porch light and peek through the curtain. My neighbors George and Monique are standing hand in hand, smiling.

Skye, they say in unison when I open the door.

I do not know what to do next. No one has been inside my home since I moved in. I haven't considered what it must look like to another. After George set up my cable, I've only spoken to them when we pass on the tight sidewalk outside our homes, always in shadows.

I turn from them and run my eyes over my belongings. The *Scrabble* board lays propped up on the wooden table. The chess set is stashed beside a neat line of books on a tall shelf.

Would you like to come in? I ask.

I hope it's okay we stopped over, George says.

Of course. Though I am not sure if this is true.

Beneath my three bulbs—instead of the usual feeble light of the streetlamps—they seem new to me. They are older than I assumed. Monique's hair is dyed a soft blonde, and George has faded tattoos on his dark forearms.

What a beautiful place, Monique says. I don't know what she means. The longer they stand here, the longer I see my home through their eyes—basic and neat, sterile.

George moves toward my table. *I love* Scrabble. *Looks like someone is winning*, he says.

Yes, I say. *Can I get you anything?* I ask.

That would be lovely, Monique says. I see a quick look pass between George and her.

While I busy myself in the exposed kitchen, I hear George's footsteps as he lumbers over to my bookcase. I hum to cut the silence.

We just came over to share a bit of mixed news with you, he says.

Yes, I say. I pour three glasses of milk and carry them to the table, then hum louder. I set out three plates, each with a slice of bread.

Let's sit, I say. They do, and I flush with what must be maternal feelings, though they are more than twice my age.

Monique runs a finger over the crust of her bread. *George got a new job out of town*, she says. *We're putting the house on the market.*

He stares at his plate like his neck is stuck.

We wanted you to be one of the first to know, she says. *Since there will be a lot of activity outside, potentially.*

We'll miss being your neighbors, George says to his plate.

I nod and keep on nodding. I take tiny bites and chew so I won't have to respond. I hear Monique's stomach grumble, though she does not raise the bread to her lips.

We're going to miss you, Monique says.

When they exit, they wave timidly at the door. Their glasses of milk remain untouched. I allow a few breaths to pass, then I pick up Monique's tumbler and shatter it against the wall. I turn George's over in my hands, smash it against the table, cutting my palm. I stomp to the bathroom sink, fingers dripping blood and milk. Nobody ever stays.

I want to show you something, Andy says. It is an hour before opening and the bread is already in the case.

He touches my shoulder, signaling me to follow. Through the kitchen, still pristine. A kettle gleams as if on display. Cabinets two feet deep, made of old stained wood, swallow up the right side of the room in the back. There's a door straight ahead, I assume leading to the alleyway where he says a raccoon family lives.

Real sweet, he says. *Two big ones and a few little ones. One of the big ones has three legs, loves bread.*

He spins to his left, opens his arms to gesture at a door. *Here we are,* he says. I can feel cold seeping out of the gaps. Brown paint peels at the edges. Above is a plastic sign with the words *NOT AN EXIT* printed in bold.

Are you ready? he asks.

For what? I ask.

But he doesn't answer. He takes my hand, twists the knob, and the cold and dark are damp as a cave.

Don't worry, he says. *Just follow me. It's worth it. I won't let you trip.*

He stands in front of me and I put both of my hands on his shoulders. He walks forward so carefully into the shadows that I feel as if we move through water. Time acts oddly—simultaneously speeds up and slows, my heart hammering.

You doing okay? he asks.

I have not been alone with a man like this ever. The light from the kitchen behind us now feels lewdly distant, though it is only a few feet away. I sense his body turning and now we are going down a different hallway, the light leaving us. He stops short. The muscles of his shoulders shift as his hands search in the black. Then I hear another knob twist, a door open. I hear his hand brushing against a wall and then the flip of the switch, the light from a bulb above us flickering and then settling into a delicate glow, illuminating framed posters and purple carpet.

Can I take you to the movies? he asks.

For weeks Andy sneaks me into the movie theatre at 3:00 AM. We finish *The Lion King* and return to his quiet kitchen.

Tell me about Skye, I say.

He laughs. *You're Skye,* he says.

It's 5:00 AM, an hour before opening. He sits on a wooden stool in the corner.

You know what I mean, I say.

He looks past me. *Her name wasn't Skye. It was Star. She was my daughter. But not quite.*

I stay silent.

His lips tighten. *I've never told anyone this,* he says.

I want to stop him. I am no one.

Andy, I say.

I lost both of them, he says.

I don't speak. If the death of my family has taught me anything, it is that grief demands silence. It refuses questions from others. I move toward him, stand at his side.

Let's open, he eventually says, clapping his hands together. I notice the deep smell of the bread for the first time, and I can't imagine how dark the loaves must look sitting in his two tiny ovens.

Andy, I say.

No, you need to go home. The sun is coming.

It is the cruelest thing anyone has said to me lately, though it's also true that few have spoken to me these past years.

I need to tell you a secret, Andy says. He holds both of my hands in his. *I am not who I seem to be.*

The night is ending and a deep purple is filling the sky. He has forgiven me for bringing up his daughter last week, or has forced himself to. I hear the twittering of a bird I can't name.

He says, *I'm everything I've told you I am. Except one thing. I didn't know how to tell you. I still don't.* He lets go of my hands, walks to the cabinets in the back of the kitchen, opens up one of the doors. His fingers tremble. *I don't know how to bake bread. It's delivered frozen. I thaw it.*

I see that the cabinet is empty.

He says, *I have no skills other than fishing, and I can't go near the water again. Please understand. Understand I didn't want to lie to you.*

This puzzle of him and water, it has never been uttered. I ask nothing, say nothing. He sits on the countertop, the gleaming metal, and waits, his loneliness blue-scented.

From the other side of this cramped kitchen, I note for the first time the fine lines at his eyes, the stubble under his chin. I study his posture, the way his shoulders slump forward, the trivial curve at the back of his neck.

I'll teach you, I finally say.

What?

I'll teach you how to bake bread.

The making of bread. The thing that killed my family.

To love a man and not know him—this is a freedom. I never wonder about secrets, because the fact of his secrets is obvious, naked.

When my family died, an improbable amount of smoke rose into the pines. It blocked the sun until a gust of wind came, and the sun showed her generous face.

There were sounds—my family's screams—and I could not tell my brother's from my mother's from my father's. All that existed was sun, smoke, fire.

Only Ash knows my shortcomings that day. And now Ash has receded, so my past is wholly mine.

Andy drapes his arm around me. My cheek rests on his shoulder. In our movie theatre, the walls are black and thick. Nothing can know we are here, warmed under three blankets. We watch *Groundhog Day*, and when it ends, Andy gets up and walks into the projection booth, puts on *Jurassic Park*.

Outside, the sun is elsewhere. I know I will meet the light again, but for now, I rest in the flickering dark, in a stranger's arms. A hero runs from something offscreen. I glance over at Andy, who has fallen asleep.

My Medusa

When I swam out of the ocean, my left hand was a jellyfish, its tentacles my fingers. Its bell my palm. I wrapped my beach towel around my body and ran home.

I am a woman accustomed to dark moods. But here I became terrified. I closed the shutters. I locked the door, counted my canned vegetables with my right hand.

It did not need water, nor did it need food. The thing needed nothing but my life for it to thrive. Weeks swept by and its tentacles danced a tango at all hours.

Work called. I told my boss I severely burned my face, so he let me be. Didn't even follow up. The coward.

I tried to research online, though all I got was fairytales, aquariums, a thousand tattoos, lonely boys drawing naked women with gills.

I wanted to trace the jellyfish's origin, its birth on my body, but each movement before its appearance had been no different than the last. I had labored, eaten, shopped, dreamed the same as always.

A jellyfish is without a heart, a brain. Without lungs. No blood, no bone. And the longer it twisted on my arm, the more I also became deprived of a heart. Lacking a mind. When I woke gasping from my nightmare, I knew. How could I not try?

The lake near the top of the mountain is quiet. Often, I am below ice thick enough that there is no risk of being seen. I have many friends here. Fish, the moon. Orion, depending on the season.

Did you know the moon will answer back if you are gracious, engaging? I purse my blue lips to the lake's surface and call his name. *Yes*, he says. *Hello old friend. I have so much to say.*

No Eyes for Them

I.

It was not so unpleasant, to be without him. We had married, and we had loved each other for maybe a year, and then we became unknown to one another. But more than that, I resented him for the things I learned after his death. They made the loss of him much easier.

But with his death there was a much greater loss. The adoption agency thought perhaps not, what with me being newly widowed.

I am not a forgiving person. I have never been. I hold close an extensive list of childhood resentments—from the playground to the tiny chapel Sunday school rooms. It's quite possibly the worst thing about me, at least out of those sins I'm aware of. It makes the grounds of my relationships pitted. It comes out sideways in the bite of my voice when I say *Good morning*. In the turn of my body—away, always spun away. I tried to be better, and then he took—with his death—my almost son. I had already learned the child's name.

It is not good to hear a name.

It is worse, even more, to see a face.

He had pink skin. He had brown eyes. Has. He has these things. But he'll never be mine. William. The name of kings.

II.

My dead husband left me a decent amount of money. It had been one of the things that made us strangers—his persistent need to take and take. He seemed—I'll regret saying this—a little soulless. Some nights, his face tense even in sleep, I considered getting out of bed and printing everything off, all his research. Who would I tell? How could I tell? Widows. So many newly widowed women, usually wealthy and quite bewildered. He found them, charmed them, and then sold their land. *I know this is overwhelming*, he'd say to them. *I can take care of everything for you. Here's my card. We'll get you into a smaller place with a rose garden, one by the sea. This house is far too large for you now.*

Now that I am the woman in black, supposedly mourning her lost husband, the wealth seems foul. I'm unable to leave the house, this house of two stories joined by a stone staircase. I lie on the marble and watch light hit the chandelier. Sometimes I make tea, listen to the birds and doze off. No one bothers me much about it—those few people in my life. In-laws. The neighbors. My book group. They think I am at home crying over him. I am not.

Perhaps soon another real estate agent from his old office will call me up, offer their help, tell me the house must feel oppressive, what with all its rooms and full baths.

William, and before him, the miscarriages. Each after I had seen the sonograms. Seen their shadowed bodies shift in murky gray.

I can barely say the things my husband did, the things I learned. It's enough just to keep from digging up his grave, dumping him out into the watery deep. He deserves no rest, but I haven't told a soul. I keep the truth as close to me as a talisman.

On January 19th, the talisman brings me no luck.

III.

I awoke that day, and the air was a smidge colder. Everything felt stagnant, quieter. Like the dial on the world was turned down. I had been widowed two months. I'd found out the truth of my husband after one week. My body was not adjusted to the betrayal. Every movement—rising, bathing, opening the blinds—was an exercise in will.

I washed my face, changed my shirt. I ordered my groceries. I ordered everything those days. There was no need to go anywhere. My toothpaste and toilet paper and apples all came to the door.

I laid on the carpet and waited for time to be over with.

When I tell the truth of what happened, I do not believe myself fully. Even as I lived it, I doubted it. An hour passed, my stomach growled. Then my doorbell rang.

IV.

I have never felt comfortable with my own mind. When I was younger, I was always alone. My mother was depressed enough that she might as well not have been there, and my father was often ill. No. Hungover. My father was often hungover. Which is a type of illness, I guess. But I lacked sympathy when he cussed the finches on late afternoons. He would not let me leave the house.

That amount of isolation plays with the psyche. I had much time to think and not a lot to do. My thoughts became warped. I tried to rid myself of the dark thoughts by staying busy—but I could only clean the kitchen so many times. The counters gleamed like a flattened jewel.

I thought I heard the radio sometimes. I often picked at my face like a scab, pulled out my hair, strand by strand, made intricate plans to run away, packed my bag, unpacked it. I became elaborately afraid of the dark, at the age of sixteen.

I met my late husband at the age of nineteen. In a way, maybe, he saved me when he took me out of that house.

No, I cannot give him that.

In all things, I've been unable to trust myself. When I discovered I was allergic to strawberries, I ate more strawberries. When Timothy, the boy a few houses down, tried to make friends, I told him I was contagious and dangerous. I have had years to cultivate my self-destructive tendencies into a type of blunt weapon held to my own neck.

I was not bent on being happy. I was not excited about the living. What was there to love in my childhood's milky walls—where out of the plaster came a faint, false broadcast? I was so lonely, I heard laughter, indistinct and absolutely imaginary.

V.

I lived alone with my late husband's secrets.

January 19th, the doorbell rang. I got up off the floor and

walked to the window. The house sat at the end of the road, where cars rarely drove, unless they'd made a wrong turn. I saw a delivery van out on the curb. I saw the boxes sitting on my doorstep. I did not see the deliveryman.

It had always been the same deliveryman, and his movements were so routine that any variation felt profound. Between those boxes and that van, I saw no one. I walked quickly to the coat stand and grabbed a jacket. I ran my fingers through my hair, why exactly, I'm not sure. When I opened the door, the van was driving away, its license plate dusty and unreadable.

This might not seem significant, but it is everything. It is the moment I lost the life I had never loved.

VI.

January 20th, I ordered more groceries. I did not need the grains and rice, but I needed to see the deliveryman.

Doctors say when we don't want to see something, we don't see it. They've done studies. They have their neat little explanations and anecdotes, though I don't think they've quite discovered the thing that happened with me, not that I would ever tell on myself.

It could have been a type of protection, psychologically speaking, though that's not the best explanation. Because in a very real sense, it left me profoundly exposed.

The doorbell rang. I looked out, saw no one. I watched the van, watched it rumble awake and then begin to move away from the curb, the driver's seat empty. I ran outside barefooted, yelling for it to come back, but my voice was weak from lack of use. I tiptoed carefully into my house, sat on the floor, and wept.

VII.

There must have been something redeemable in my personality. I was not entirely a lost cause. Hope wasn't the thing that saved me. I had no hope. Nor was it religion. Or reverence for nature or life or any such thing.

If I think back on it now, I believe it was just an animal will to live. An instinct to keep going, as miserable and wretched as I was.

Which does not account for my redemption. But again, there was something animal about that, too.

VIII.

The next day, after the van had driven away with no driver, I ordered more groceries. Hundreds of dollars' worth. Heavy things. Sodas and frozen steaks and kindling. I pulled a lawn chair from the backyard to the front stoop. I set it up with a modest table and a water pitcher. I wanted to look casual. Normal. I even laid a newspaper in my lap.

Another instinct is to freeze in the face of danger.

The van drove up without a driver. It parked on its own volition. The back door opened, and boxes moved through the air and were placed on a trolley that was pulled out of the back by no one. The trolley moved down the drive smoothly, like water.

Morning, said no one.

I cannot know for sure how my face looked, but my body went hard and fixed. If an earthquake had hit at that second, I might've toppled over and shattered like glass.

Can I leave these inside your door? Or do you want them on your stoop like normal? said the air.

I started to cry.

Well, look here. Are you okay? Is everything okay? said the nothing.

The boxes on their trolley waited in front of me. The air felt warmer. I could hear the nothing clear its throat.

Ma'am, do you need anything? Are you hurt?

I can only imagine what that moment was like for him. I don't even know how much time passed. It must have been very difficult for him to decide what to do with his hands, the hands I could not see on the body that did not exist. He did not reach out and touch me. Nor did he say another word.

After the boxes were stacked at my feet, I heard him take a deep breath, and then the trolley moving toward the van again. It bumped along against nothing. I heard a bit of clanging as it was put away and the van doors were shut.

I knew enough to know that ghosts don't drive, hold jobs, try to comfort widows. I knew enough to recognize I had gone mad.

IX.

I went to sleep then for what felt like days. I think it was days, though I can't be certain. The boxes of groceries, left outside, grew soggy with rain.

Over the next month, I ate everything in the house. Even the old raisins in the back of the cupboard. I finished off the big-ticket whiskey. It gave me a halo of amber and then it gave me another long sleep.

When all the food was gone, my stomach hurt, then cramped, then I grew dizzy with hunger. I could not decide what to do. The landscaped nothingness provided only dandelions. It had been a good while since I had gone to a store. I was scared I might cry in the aisles from the lights and noise.

I ordered Chinese food. A sedan drove up within the hour, and when a small woman came out with a plastic bag my eyes filled with tears. I was so happy to see her. I over-tipped and she even laughed a little in thanks and then drove away and I saw it all. I saw her the whole time.

X.

My husband had been a monster. The marriage didn't look bad. It didn't even feel bad. Just loveless. Just fire hazard dry. I already knew he was a type of liar. I just didn't know the whole of it. When you bury a man, he can't protect his secrets. All the doors unlock with the right key.

XI.

After a week of Chinese food, I ordered more groceries. I watched from the window as the van came and the boxes moved through the air like leaves on a breeze.

After the van drove away—on its own, without a driver—I slipped on shoes and staggered out of my yard for the first time in months. The birds seemed loud. The sun felt offensive, though the sky was a bit overcast.

I came up on the closest house, a block from mine. A pickup truck sat in the driveway. No lights were on. Up ahead I saw two women power walking. They reminded me of ducks, waddling fast but getting nowhere really. They had sweatbands around their wrists. One raised her hand to me, and I waved back. This is what it is to be part of the world again, I thought.

The women turned down another way. Now the birds actually sounded nice. I sauntered past more houses, humming to myself low, following the women's path.

A lawnmower started up, and I saw the women wave to the lawnmower. The lawnmower began to move, though no one pushed it, and the women walked on and I watched a neat line in the grass form.

I must have screamed. The women spun around and the lawnmower halted in its path. I turned on my heels and ran home, never looking back.

XII.

I went out at night from then on, after the cars were in the garages and people were seated at their television sets. I peeked into windows. A girl played alone with a stuffed doll in her room. A woman washed dishes. Everywhere rooms hummed with the movements of women.

At the close of Jackson Street, a road ending in a white three-story, I found a window dull with light. The blinds were pulled tight, but at one edge were two inches of bare glass. I crept into the flowerbed and peered in. A woman was naked and moving. Candlelight flickered. Her hands grasped at air. She sat up on her elbows—legs spread wide—and her tongue reached for nothing. She threw back her head, exposing her neck. She appeared delicate and raw, insane, submitting to a thing unseen.

A candle floated from the nightstand and hovered over her. She laughed and turned on her stomach, stuck her ass in the air. She rocked back and forth, unhurried. The candle tipped and wax fell on her back.

I could not see the man that moved with her, for her.

I could not see any man. I could not tell where they existed. Except for what fell against and with their bodies. By those impressions, I knew the men were there.

XIII.

I surrendered, in a way. I did not fight it, did not try too hard to understand it, but my walks stretched further, and I crept into many yards and over fences. I did not miss seeing the grown men, the husbands and fathers and even the teenagers. But the babies, I wanted to tap on the glass and ask the mothers to bring their nothing near so I could smell and touch and listen.

This new grief knew no limits. Now every baby boy had been taken from me, not only my William, not only my unnamed.

XIV.

In the guest closet I make a little shrine of boy's clothes for William. Sitting on the floor, I hum and laugh as I rearrange the sleeves of a blue button-down. It looks as if a ghost turns toward me, a ghost hugs me, a ghost sleeps in my lap. I run a toy truck over the undusted wood panels. For a moment, I think I hear William laugh with me.

What kind of man poisons his wife? I thought the glass of water my husband had served me each morning was for nothing but thirst. He was cocky enough to write the recipe out, leave it in his desk to discover after his death.

All my lost sons.

XV.

I run at night. There's a moon out so pink and large it looks like a mistake.

I only hear my sneakers hitting pavement. There's not even wind to rustle the pines. I'm out of shape and stop to catch my breath just outside my neighborhood's entrance, where the words *Garden Village* gleam in rich moonlight.

There's a snap, like a twig breaking, but a large twig, and I go still as a deer, barely breathing. Then I sigh, annoyed with myself—my weak, scared self.

I turn to the familiar streets, run past my sleeping neighbors. There's a tightness on my arm. I am tugged to the pavement kicking my legs and my legs strike something and there's a pressure over my lips and I try to bite the suffocating air. My wrists are now held together behind me and I am splayed on the road. Gravel in my cheek, and I cannot get my teeth around the weight on my mouth. Something is on the backs of my knees.

There's the sound of the car before I see the lights, but when the lights sweep over my body the pressure disappears and I am left sobbing in the middle of the street, curled up tight as a rosebud.

The car brakes in front of me, the door swings open and all I can hear is, *Are you okay? Are you okay?* It's a man's voice. *Are you okay?*

I cannot see this man who has saved me and I start to sob harder. I feel a light touch on my shoulder and shudder. The touch recedes and I hear his voice near the car, *Yes, yes, just past the entrance of Garden Village. An attack. A young woman. Yes, I'm staying with her.*

Below the unbearable stars, my arms with shallow scratches, my being more vulnerable than if I were opened up on a surgeon's rack—this is the moment, the moment everything changes.

XVI.

The next hours are a sort of hell. I sit in a plastic chair in the sheriff's office and answer questions spoken by nothing. I am given a blanket and tea. When I'm asked, a third time, if I can describe the perpetrator, I laugh. I can't help myself. The clock says 1:40 AM.

Is he still here? I ask the air.

Who?

The man who saved me, I say.

Why?

Are you questioning him?

The officer's radio crackles.

We already did, says the nothing.

But is he still here? I say.

He's still here. He wanted to stick around. Did he have anything to do with this?

No, no, I say. *Can I see him?*

XVII.

In the home of my dead husband, I turn on all the lights. Then I change my mind and call the man again.

XVIII.

It is not that I was saved. It is not that I was belly down in need, and he came to rescue me. Not exactly.

When you learn a man by only his touch, his voice, his scent, you understand him differently. I have grown a sixth sense. This is how it feels to be safe.

He asks why I never look him in the eyes.

I only let him take me out at night. He drives us to Mud Lake. There are enough stars to fill several skies. He smells not unlike the pines, the air before it rains.

My dress rests on a wet rock. Around my wrists are many bracelets. I am ankle deep in muck. Cold swallows my hips. Soon I will acclimate.

I do not know how we can go on this way, the secret of my blindness intact.

But for tonight, I see the outline of his body in the water. It rushes from him as he kicks further out into the depths. The lake cuts away from the trace of his shoulders. I hear it stir as he turns back to me, calls me by my name.

In this moment, no past haunts me. The worst of me, the worst of what I've lived, is swallowed up in the dark's damp silence. In this moment, with the wet silhouette of a body of a man, I am known.

Tastes Like Rat

The blobs of Oakville, Wash., are alive—or at least they were once alive, or part of some living creature... The mystery blobs, half the size of rice grains, have appeared twice during rainfall...

—"Mystery blobs were once alive,"
The New York Times, August 20, 1994

In his sleep, he unfurled his fists. He parted his cracked lips. My hand on his chest, his breath was nothing but a whisper. He twitched as if a thing hunted him.

Next door, Meredith McGrath weeded her overgrown flower garden. I sat up in bed and watched through the window. A streetlight shone aggressively on her house. Her yellow hat bobbed up and down over her stout two-foot hedge. Every few minutes she'd wipe at her eyes with a soiled glove. She lifted a shoebox to the sky. She was not weeding. She was burying her cat. *TIGER* was written in blocky letters on the side, next to a Nike swoosh.

Meredith looked up over that low border and through the unclean glass. She stared straight at me, unblinking. I think. The lights inside the bedroom had burned out. Perhaps she was only considering her own mud-marked face.

...

The sky had fallen twice in Oakville. Slick blobs, like jellyfish. Making the town, the pets, the songbirds ill. Lying beside him, reunited after my final semester, I should have been full of celebration, my heart sparking. But when he coughed, his throat rattled. For three days he'd been without color, as if his skin was dissolving. He said no one was coming to help.

They think we are mad, he said. *They know we are poor.*

I didn't doubt this. I called the far-off hospital anyhow and when I said the town was sick, I heard a sigh and then a dial tone. Like I was pranking them. I called 911 and it was the same. I called the doctor, but the voicemail was full.

Outside, a blue jay fell from the sky.

The next day he started to bruise. Wounds grew by the hour, like the boundary lines of countries blurring.

My body hurt in places unnoticed before, unnamed. When I moved near his body, something ached bone-silent and lonely. The thing in him snaked through my fingers into my belly. On the morning of the fifth day, I stepped from the shower. The blood from my thighs was as thick and formed as a man-of-war. Knees buckling, I muttered a neglected prayer, like muscle memory. I threw out the bathroom mat, changed my mind, and burned it in the yard. My beloved slept.

We were two sallow sweethearts on a sea of salted sheets, floating through fever and shadows. We ate each other's laments. A sun came up, snickering at the heat it spilled into that illicit sickroom.

We could hide from nothing, especially the moon, who made us nauseous, and thirsty, and a little savage. Who stayed past its welcome. I pulled the blinds, but when I turned my back, they were peeled away again and I would clutch them together then lie on the sea exhausted and still he slept and still the sun fell about mocking and tapping at the glass. I would say we ate, but I am not convinced that's true. If he awoke it was only to ask to be held.

Days later, I saw Meredith McGrath's yellow hat bob up and down. Up and down. She kissed the dirt-stained shoebox, then tucked it under her arm, carried it into her house through her backdoor. It began to rain.

I continued to birth those dark bellies of red, yet I refused to tell him. He suffered with a beast I could not reach.

Away, he said in his sleep.

Nothing answered back.

Leave, he said.

The moon patted his head, pulled at the blood of me.

I could occasionally hear traffic. Once an airplane. The doorbell rang. Boots shuffled away.

I woke with Tiger on my stomach—curled up, purring. When she felt me shift, she stretched forward and licked my cheek, her tongue tough and warm.

I'm thirsty, said the cat.

I have no milk, I said.

You have blood, said the cat.

Tiger followed me to the kitchen. I held onto the cold furniture as I made my way through the cramped rooms. I filled the ivory porcelain bowl, the one belonging to my beloved's mother.

Thank you, said the cat.

Do you need anything else? I asked.

Yes, said the cat. *I would like a bed*.

So I cut my hair off using kitchen shears. I wove a bed and placed it beside the stove.

Anything else? I asked.

Yes, she said. *I would like a rat*.

So I chopped off my big toes and placed them in a trap.

That will be all, said the cat.

I nodded, struggled back to the bedroom and slept.

In the morning the man I loved was gone. I dragged myself through the home whispering his name. In the hall, in a small square of the sun, Tiger rolled onto her back.

Good morning, she said.

Good morning, I said. *Have you seen him?*

Good morning, she repeated. *I had such a pleasant night*.

That is nice, I said. *Have you seen the one I love?*

I drank and slept and ate, she said. *My belly is very full*.

That is nice, I said. *I am looking for him. I must lay with him*.

I'll tell you where he is, said the cat. *But only if you give me something more to drink*.

I crawled into the kitchen and fetched the ivory bowl. I saw the trap was sprung. The kitchen was clean of blood and bone.

The cat drank and drank from the bowl of my blood.

Are you still thirsty? I said.

More, said the cat.

I filled it again.

More, she said.

I was not feeling well.

I said, *Please, have you seen my beloved? He looks sickly, but he is very handsome and he has hair the color of the chestnut tree.*

It is going to rain, said the cat.

I am seeking him, I said.

I will tell you where he is, said the cat, *but first I must go out and dance in the rain.*

No, I said. I was angry then.

I know many dances, said the cat. *Look.* The cat stood on her back legs.

You will starve without me, I said.

The cat chuckled at this.

Look at me, she said. *I dance so well.*

I will tell your mother, I said.

Watch my hips, she said. *The tomcats always say* yes.

She swung her hips, and I must say, she looked very beautiful, like a go-go dancer, scarlet-lipped. She shimmied out into the yard, where the fourth rain fell. It gummed on her shoulders like fat jewels. Her mouth opened. She was speaking to me, but I couldn't make the words out over the sound of the laughing moon.

Gekker

Beneath a half sun, the woman gave birth to a girl with yellow eyes, long fingers, and a fox's tail. The midwife said nothing as she wrapped the child in a blanket. The father turned his head, walked out into the field and beat his fists against the mud.

They named her Amaris. She never bit her mother's breast or woke her parents while they slept. She certainly did not throw her toys.

The father and the mother, by and by, overlooked her fox's tail, and Amaris was gentle, so good, and she chased the neighborhood kids around trees, tripped over her own feet. It brought the families joy to watch her play.

The mother later had three boys, each a year apart. Amaris would sneak into the boys' room and groom them with her tongue. At daybreak, they were often found nestled in her tail.

By the time she grew into a long-lashed girl of sixteen years, everyone accepted her as she was, everyone but Loomis.

Loomis—red haired, pigeon-toed, fifteen years old—thought Amaris was of the devil, or perhaps she was the devil. His father, the town's pastor, did not put this idea in Loomis's head. In fact,

Pastor Wade thought Amaris was a fine girl, a great example of godliness, what with her impeccable manners, dedication to family, and natural gift for making cupcakes from scratch. Plus, when she sang, the birds grew silent to hear her.

Amaris knew how Loomis felt about her. She had a good instinct for that sort of thing. Also, he'd told her, which made things quite clear.

I don't like you, he said to her one day when she was alone and sitting below a weeping willow.

Is that so? she said.

It most certainly is, he said.

Have I done something to harm you? she asked. *If I did, I apologize.*

Loomis didn't like this answer. This was manipulation, devil-talk.

It's not one thing you done, he said. *I know who you are. You are not of God.*

Amaris found this rather harsh. She squirmed a little under his stare. She would have liked to have defended herself, but she didn't know how to respond, because no one had ever spoken to her like that. She'd never heard those words said to anybody, in fact.

She got her mouth working again, was about to tell him he was wrong, but he turned his gangly body, started hobbling along the path, whistling and tossing a small rock up and down.

Loomis doesn't like me, Amaris said to her mother and father at the dinner table.

Her three brothers exchanged looks.

Now what makes you think that? her father asked. He was reaching over her glass for more bread, dropping crumbs in her lemonade.

He told me I am not of God, she said.

Her father's face became apple red. Her mother slammed her fork on her plate.

Bullshit, her mother said.

Loomis is a troubled boy, her father said. *His mother left with that lion tamer, remember? Hasn't been right since.*

It's true, her mother said. *That was hard on him. Harder on him than on his father. Pastor Wade doesn't have to be so secretive about the milkmaid these days. A bit secretive. But not as much.*

The three brothers were snickering and pinching each other under the table.

Roar! said the youngest boy to the oldest boy.

Anyhow, her father said. *You are of God. You are closer to an angel than any other girl I'll ever know.*

You're my father. You have to talk nice, she said.

Actually, I really don't, he said and laughed. *But the truth is the truth.*

Sure is, said her mother.

That night, while Amaris did the dishes, she thought about the devil. His long tongue and thick thighs. Two black horns sharp as lightening. And eyes that rolled around in their sockets, as if untethered. The devil was, of course, handsome—this wicked one, dark dragon, prince of the world.

She looked out at the moon, which was very full of itself. She left the dishes undone and walked onto the porch.

Mother, she said. *Why do I have a fox's tail?*

Her mother stopped rocking in her chair and lowered her book.

Because God made you special, her mother said.

Do fox tails run in the family? she said.

Heavens, no, her mother said. *Listen. You are one of a kind. And we love you that way.*

Do you know anyone else like me? Have you heard of anyone?

Her mother thought for a moment.

Well, there is talk of a boy out by Mud Lake who sheds his skin like a snake.

This did not make Amaris feel any better. She went back inside and finished cleaning the kitchen.

When summer came, the three brothers built a treehouse in a hemlock's branches. Inside they crafted stools, four of them, because their sister was forever and always welcome. They had a table for cards, and a glossy card set, and a crate where they kept apples and melons.

One day, while they were all in the treehouse, and the weather was especially wild—lots of rain and wind—they heard someone huffing and puffing up the ladder. They saw the flair of Loomis's red hair first, and then his eyes—beady, searching.

He heaved himself up onto the floor and stood awkwardly, his hands in his pockets. He glanced behind at the ground twelve feet below. The three brothers paused their whittling, and Amaris stopped licking her tail.

I want to talk to your sister, he said.

No, said the oldest brother.

Go away, said the middle brother.

Roar! said the youngest.

It's okay brothers, she said.

Privately, said Loomis.

As you wish, she said, and followed him down the ladder.

They walked together to a small patch of clover, away from her brothers' ears.

I've been thinking, Loomis said. *I've been thinking it's time that you go.*

Is that so? she said.

Yes, he said. *I'll help you get everything together that you need. Make sure that you have supplies and a map and a route, at least the beginning of one.*

Is that so? she said again.

He was earnest, and sure of his conviction. He did not see the way her eyes narrowed, how one side of her mouth lifted into a hint of a smirk. She thumped her tail against the weeds. He kept prattling on about the best way for her to trek into the mountains, the kind of boots that would benefit her. He was God's solider. He would rid the town of her, but he would be humane about it. She'd stopped listening. She was looking closely at his hands, how the sun hit them, how they appeared wet.

What do you say? he said.

Sure, she said, though what she had agreed to, she had no idea.

Wonderful. You've made the right choice. I'll fetch you tomorrow.

And off he went, over the hill, back to his home, the home without a mother, the home where God's chosen boy slept.

After dinner that night, Amaris sat by herself in the treehouse, listening to nothing. The corners grew dark while Amaris thought about fate, thought about the difference between a body and a

soul, about why a God would see her mother's womb, and the
girl growing there, and decide, with a gesture of His hand, to
make her a bit of a dog. What did it mean that she told small
lies? That the holes in the yard were made by her, not by moles?
That she hungered for rabbit, raw and freshly caught? That she
found birds—those snatched from their nests—tasted best beneath
moonlight? The thinking made her tired, and she fell asleep in
the tree, while bats flew out to catch their kill, and wild poppies
closed to the evening's black.

She awoke to the noise of someone on the ladder—someone
wheezing, struggling. She could see the weak dawn through the
planks. She stretched her arms and her tail and popped her head
down to see Loomis straddling the ladder.

Are you okay? she asked.

Yes, he said, stopping a moment to catch his breath. *I'm just
tired. I was up all night praying.*

Well that seems silly, she said. *You only have to tell God
something once.*

Says the devil, he said.

She laughed, a deep sound in her throat, a warning—primal,
instinctive. She knew by the sun that her family was still in bed,
that the grass and tree were slick with dew, that Loomis had traded
sleep—so necessary for a growing boy—for her surrender, which
was not forthcoming, ever. In one hand he hauled a pair of pink
boots and a backpack bursting with food. He reached the final
rung, and tried to sling his haul up ahead of him onto the room's
floor. Then he fell.

He didn't cry out when he hit the ground. By the time Amaris was at his side, his eyes were closed and blood seeped out from the back of his head where a small stone rested. She pulled him into her lap, wrapped her tail around his waist, licked his wound.

His skin was cool to her tongue. She lapped the blood away, and beneath the blood she found an orange skin. She groomed his neck and found bright rust dotted with small spots. Gently, she pulled off his t-shirt. He whimpered in her arms. As she cleaned his back, she uncovered large inky stains like eyes. His skin felt rough. She turned his face to hers. He was crying, his pupils wide. She licked them, and they became two dark beads. He smelled like the sun. She heard her brothers calling. She took the nape of his neck in her teeth and dragged him deep into the trees.

Days Come Around Again

I'm reading the obituaries when this guy sits down next to me, starts feeding the pigeons. Or tries to feed the pigeons. He's throwing large chunks of beef jerky. The smell is strong, even in the open air of the park.

Here, pigeon, pigeon, he says. He clucks his tongue.

I have two of the dead left to read about, but I can't concentrate with all this jerky being tossed.

That's meat, I say.

The man turns to me, slower than you'd think. *No, it's not*, he says. *This is bread.*

I clear my throat, nod. Go back to the obituaries, but out of the corner of my eye I can tell he's still looking my way.

It's bread, he says again.

I nod, keep my head down.

I said it's bread. He sounds angry, or like he's about to cry.

I begin to gather my things, but I spot my ex across the lawn. Every day I come here hoping to catch a glimpse of her, but now that she's here, I realize this is a bad idea. She pays for a hotdog. She's got a jean skirt on.

That bird's name is Noah, the man says. He's pointing at the ground, at nothing.

Yes, I say.

Yes, he says.

My ex is walking away with the hotdog. She moves toward the parking lot.

Excuse me, I say, stand and rock on my heels. I don't know why I am the way I am, but I say, *Noah is dead.*

No, he says.

Yes, I say.

The man sucks on his teeth. He gives me a glance, then continues throwing jerky.

That one there, that's Kyle, the man says.

Yes, I say. *I knew a man named Kyle.* I see my ex pulling onto the one-way street. Her windows are tinted but I know the car, I know her, I know more than I should.

Yes, he says.

He was not a good man, I say.

Yes, he says.

I sit back down, face him with my whole body. It's not like I don't have all the time in the world nowadays.

Tell me more, I say. *Tell me about the men you've known.*

Tell Us Our Names

I hit rock bottom in Poulsbo, Washington. My career as a pet psychic had stalled. I had one good eye, two good hands, little else. Herbert, my business partner, died. I lived at his one-bedroom apartment, alongside the coked-up couple next door. Where else was I to go? Couldn't get the sink fixed. Couldn't get the mice out. I thought staying put would save me.

Herbert kept visiting. I'd wake up in the middle of the night and he'd be at the foot of my bed, just as shimmery and wispy as any ghost in the movies. Those Hollywood people got that shit accurate, I tell you what.

Julie, he'd say.

Get lost, Herbert. It's 1:00 AM, I'd say.

Julie, don't be like that, he'd say.

This would go on. He really liked to mess with my sleep.

I swear to God, I'd say. He'd stand over my bed.

You have to listen to me, he'd say. *You got it all wrong, your technique with the animals. Especially the cats. It's different. You have to do it differently. No offense.*

Maybe he had a point. I'd been off my game the last year or so. Or maybe I'd been off always. Kittens hadn't made it. More than once. No one wants to hire a pet psychic who can't keep kittens alive. Then that turtle. Lord help me, that turtle. I thought it wanted sun, freedom. But now I suspect it just wanted appreciation.

Herbert, you have to get these mice out, I'd say.

I'm here to save your career, he'd say. *Listen, Julie. You have to listen to the cats. You can't keep steamrolling them.*

Tell me more in the morning, I'd say.

You can't expect to be a good pet psychic if you can't get these mice out yourself, he'd say. *Also, they aren't hurting anything. Why can't you coexist? Maybe they'll teach you something.*

Truth is, I was starting to get some faith in myself. Those mice. They talked the oddest talk, but I honed my new skill with them. I got really good.

What do you have to show me right now, mice? I'd ask.

Julie, what's the point? You never listen to us.

I do, I'd say.

You don't, they'd say. *You hear us but you don't listen. You just go on and on about yourself.*

Which was a cheap jab. You could say that about almost anyone.

What are our names? they'd say.

One evening, like all evenings, I was kind of drunk and I'd taken a white pill and three sleek pink pills. I couldn't feel my hands or feet, which was ideal. Who needs them? Ghost Herbert wasn't around. Something stroked my stomach and I looked down and it was a garter snake. One long red stripe along its body, and its eyes were glossy black, unblinking.

What are you doing with your life, Julie, it said. A statement, not a question.

It slithered up my chest, across my bare breasts. Its scales felt cold and wet.

I began to cry.

I'm lonely, I said.

The snake climbed my neck, braided itself into my hair. So tight, my scalp throbbed.

You have to choose love, the snake said.

You don't understand, I said.

Through the wall, I heard the neighbors arguing, a thud, what sounded like glass breaking. The drywall muffled the woman's scream. Outside, a car alarm went off.

Do you know God? the snake asked.

I was weeping. The woman next door was weeping.

I can show you God, the snake said.

I raised my hand to my one good eye, covered the light.

The snake's tongue tickled my ear. *Stupid Julie*, it said. *Just choose already. You're surrounded by love.*

All Our Little Ones

The children drowned on a Sunday. Three of them. All newborns. The rest of the deaths came the Sundays after.

It took us all awhile to figure out the cause of death, since none of them were around water when they drowned, except Tony, taking a bath. The others, though, they were sleeping or up in sycamores or sitting at their cramped kindergarten craft tables. Sally Shapiro was making a mud pie. George Thompson, a valentine.

By the time the FBI got involved, we had lost twenty babies and toddlers. We didn't talk of it at the time, but there were fifteen miscarriages, too. The real number is probably higher, but who wants to share these things? My grief couldn't catch up with me. Still hasn't. I went hard as rime ice.

They had lots of questions for everyone, the agents. Scribbled a lot of stuff down. Stared at us a real long time if we stumbled on our words. And the press, may they all rot in hell, even the sound guys.

My brother-in-law tried to explain it to me, how they knew it was drowning. He talked about water in the stomach and bloody froth in the airways. I got up and filled a glass from the kitchen sink and walked out of the room. I opened the sliding glass doors to the backyard and left, right into the woods in my slippers. There were a lot of women like me, going around in pajamas and unmade faces. Still are. New footpaths have formed in the forest from our wandering.

I didn't have a child to lose. My one son, Cal, was nineteen and at seminary. Three hours and fifteen minutes from my doorstep. Even then, I worried for him. I ran my fingers over his daddy's urn and prayed.

My Cal, his first word *love*. First steps, into my arms. All his years, one single tussle over a friend's honor during an away game. A damn good man, that's what they say.

And then, there were no more drownings. Within the year the FBI packed up, the press left. They called it bad forensics. A virus had run its course. Not a drowned child in the ground, save little Tony, they said. But we knew the truth. There were no more children to lose.

And why was it here? Could have been the water. Could have been the soil. But we are a fine town. We take care of each other. You've never seen a DMV line move with such finesse. Jellied candies and cookies on each counter. Never seen cows so tranquil munching their miles of bright grass. Even through the drownings we didn't gossip. We kept our doors unlocked. A lesser town would have torched itself in a fistful of days.

The knock came on a Sunday evening. I recognize my neighbors' knocks. Mrs. Gladys has a real soft one, three taps. Frank's is a persistent bang like a mechanical hammer. The UPS woman—two hard raps. This knock, though, I hadn't heard before.

Mrs. Smith? the man said, his hands grasped behind him when I answered the door. I took in his dull suit.

May he never forgive me. I slapped him. He didn't even flinch.

Mrs. Smith? he repeated, cleared his throat. *May we come in? My name is Oliver, from Roanoke Seminary. And this is Father Mack.* Behind Oliver stood a priest with a turned face.

I stepped aside.

Cal had drowned. In his bed. There was an investigation. They didn't understand yet, but they would soon.

But I knew what happened. You let the light in, and you don't run it out, it gets big and fat and happy. It spreads its greedy paws over each inch of land and love you've got.

I overturned the coffee table. I curled up fetal on the couch. Oliver, he was in no hurry. He sat on my late husband's wingback until I learned to breathe again. Father Mack hung his head. It might have been days that passed.

Can we call someone to sit with you? Oliver asked.

I moved my eyes to the urn. *I got him*, I said.

Oliver nodded, moved to leave. Father Mack walked out my door never speaking a word.

One thing, Mrs. Smith, Oliver said. He seemed small in the breezeway, his voice faint. If he hadn't been the messenger of death, I would have called his eyes kind.

He looked sideways at Father Mack's silhouette in the darkening yard. But he didn't say anything more, only lowered his gaze and left.

Oliver came to see me again. He didn't bring any gospel. Just hung out in the kitchen and examined each family photo on the fridge.

He wanted to know about Cal's life before seminary, what he had done in his free time, the types of girls he had liked. Oliver said they had been good friends, that he had learned a lot from Cal. He asked about the drowned children, too, what we knew. Which was nothing, officially speaking, and I told him as much.

I didn't mind his visit. Or the next. Or the one after that. It was nice to have someone to talk with. Oliver drove so far I made sure I fed him both meat and vegetables. He started showing up every Friday evening, and I would make Cal's old bed for him. It felt right before I knew why it should.

I knew Cal real personally. Oliver folded his hands, pushed his plate of toast aside. *Did you know that?* he asked me.

Of course, I told him. *That's why you stay in my home like a son.*

Oliver took my hand. *I loved him, was going to ask him to marry me.*

I held his gaze.

He said, *Cal knew it was coming for him. Knew it because he dreamed it. I don't know about these sorts of things. I had laughed it off.* He squared his shoulders. *Now I have dreams.*

I held a palm to his forehead. His lower lip quivered. He must have been good to Cal for it to look for him. It seeks out the purest ones first.

Get some sin in you, son. And you'll be fine, I said.

He left me there, pulled out of the driveway a little too fast, running up on the curb like a man meant to survive.

What the Body Says

I drive the dirt road when the pain nearly makes me turn into the ditch. It lasts three seconds then disappears. I'm left cussing. It came out of nowhere, like a flash flood. I don't know much about the body, but I know that's where my right ovary is. Like silence after battle, there is no more pain.

I go on with the hours. I drop off daisies for my father—laid up beneath blankets, counting the ruts in his ceiling. I buy myself groceries, wash the car. The whole time, my awareness is bent to my ovary, listening, ready if it has anything else to say.

Then a lesser pain. For weeks, it hums, sharing both sides now, the riddle. It wants, but it doesn't know my native tongue.

When Shawn touches me, he is an artist forming abstractions with his palms. But all I can think of are my ovaries, the knotty threats of them. Candles are lit. He's even put jazz on, which I find distracting but nearly lovely.

His mouth at my belly—shrill twinge. When the pain returns for its three seconds, it is so sharp, I buck and hit Shawn's teeth with my hipbone. He fumbles backwards, his lip bleeding.

I am speaking, he is speaking but neither of us can hear each other, and when I reach toward the red of his mouth, he flinches.

I hear myself saying, *My body wants something. Something. I don't know.*

And Shawn asks, *What?*

And I say, *Something is wrong with my body.*

I am doing a terrible job of making this right. He has no idea what I am talking about, and yet he still turns his head to the side, gathers me up in his arms. My body says nothing. Shawn sighs and untangles himself from me, withdraws into the bathroom.

One second, he yells over the sound of water.

Down the dirt road my father is dying. Tomorrow, he'll tell me that he feels no pain. That he feels nothing. He'll tell me a dozen lies. I will kiss his forehead and give him thanks.

Please Enjoy Going Where You Are Going

She went out on the river in her canoe, beneath a winter-shaped night. She drifted south. Yawning, trailing her fingers in the sunless water. A star fell. Georgia made a wish and closed her eyes, giving herself up to a drowsiness that was caustic, overdue. Morning arrived. She floated by stone homes and glass factories, a few marinas and one county fair where children tittered on the top of a Ferris wheel, and below them sweethearts kissed. The air smelled of cotton candy. Pop music thrummed like war beats. A clown in the trees pissed into the river.

She was just becoming sleepy again when a naked man emerged swimming beside her. Water gleamed on his shoulders.

Rebecca? he asked.

My name is not Rebecca, she said.

You look just like her, he said.

I don't know what to tell you, she said.

You do not have paddles for your canoe, he said.

I am going wherever I am going, she said.

He turned in the water and looked at the county fair. Lights strobed like a heartbeat.

I am so sorry, he said. *I must have the wrong decade.* He stared at her throat. *Are you sure you are not Rebecca?*

I am not Rebecca, she said.

He nodded. *So sorry to have bothered you. Please enjoy going where you are going,* he said and disappeared below the water.

Georgia held her fingers to her throat and touched the scar. It was a red hillock, a puckered mouth. It felt delicate, as if with just a breeze, it might rip open and bleed.

Under her canoe, he swam.

Once upon a time, a girl walked home from school in a pink dress and red shoes. She swung a patent leather purse stuffed with lip gloss and bread. She started to cross the Salt Creek Bridge and saw something she was not meant to see.

At first, she thought it was a dead, unclothed child. Then he opened his eyes and dove behind the rocks and shadows.

You cannot tell them about me, he said when he resurfaced. *Girl, you cannot tell.*

Tell who what? she asked. She liked to play dumb. It had worked for her many times, especially with boys of a certain age.

Girl, he said. *I am happy here. If you tell anyone where I am, they won't like it one lick.*

My name is not girl, she said.

What's your name then? he asked.

Wouldn't you like to know, she said.

He laughed. *Do you have anything to eat?* he asked.

Yes, she said.

Then come down, he said.

She moved without grace along the mossy ridge.

Are you going to put on clothes? she asked when she sat beside him. Their toes dangled in the lazy current.

He laughed again.

Each day after school she brought an apple, a piece of bread, and a soda. He never seemed especially hungry. He ate slowly, as if time were of no consequence. Often, as the sun grew tired, she left him nibbling on the core of a Honeycrisp.

For her, he was magic. Classrooms and recess and prayer time were nothing compared to the feel of his hand on hers. Innocent, hesitant, and warm. In him, she glimpsed something dreamlike, and it was her inability to pull it into focus that made her sure he was not of the Earth, not fully.

You're not from here, she said to him once.

No, he said. He seemed to know exactly what she meant.

Where are you from? she said.

Guess, he said.

I don't know, she said.

You'll take me there one day, he said.

A secret can hide anywhere in the body, and his secret lived in her throat. She could feel it catch when she neared him. Often, she fell mute. Together they fed small fishes their crumbs, until she noticed the failing light and ran home.

While Georgia slept in the canoe, the swimming man placed seaweed and nuts and raspberries beside her, then he blessed her hands. She was too tired to question where the food came from. She assumed the birds watched over her. Perhaps the ravens.

It was a starless sky. She was without dreams though she was in a deep sleep, so deep that she heard nothing, felt nothing, sensed only black. The canoe traveled steadily as the water moved toward the falls. He heard the roar of water hitting rocks below. He pulled her into the river and onto the shore, where she trembled from the cold.

Why? she asked.

He kissed her cheek. *Rest*, he said.

I gave you away, she said.

Be held, he said.

They came for you. I cannot be forgiven, she said.

Be warmed, he said.

He shaped a nest with pine needles and finch feathers. They drew close together and slept.

Say your name, he said.

Georgia, she said.

No, he said. *Why do you lie to me?*

Once upon a time, the naked boy did not greet her at the bridge, and she stumbled into the water calling for him. She splashed around like a caught trout. A spot of blood fell on her white dress and she looked up and saw him, trembling, in a tree. A dog had bitten his thigh.

You must go to the hospital, she said.

They cannot know about me, he said.

You'll die losing that much blood, she said.

They can't know about me, he said.

Stay there, she said.

When the dog came out of the brush, she wrestled it and trapped it in the raspberry canes. She ran to the hospital to find her aunt, the kind nurse. When they returned to the bridge, the boy was no longer in the tree. They found only a trail of blood.

Let's follow the blood, said the girl.

The boy had spoken the truth before. When the kind nurse found him behind a meaty boulder, she shook her head in sadness and said they must bring him to The Home in Port Angeles. But he was fast and lithe. The boy slipped into the water, vanishing in a bloom of red.

Once, a ghost visited the girl in her bedroom. It sat beside her on her daisy sheets.

Ghost, what have I done? asked the girl.

The ghost did not answer.

I've lost him, haven't I? said the girl. *I have driven him from his home.*

The ghost did not argue. The girl took it as a sign that she must abandon all of her memories, all of her desires, must take a new name.

On the fourth day, after they had reunited, she awoke and gathered her clothes to leave. He reached for her arm.

Do not go, he said.

I betrayed you, she said.

No, he said. *Let me show you something.*

He placed his hand over her closed eyes. She saw a life. A thousand days swimming in circles. Traveling up and down time like it was a rickety ladder. Calling her by another name. Braiding stones into the shape of her.

The fair at midnight was filled with the ghosts of laughter. She began to climb the Ferris wheel.

Where are you going? he asked.

I am going to steal a star for you, she said.

Stars can't breathe in the water, he said.

Fine, she said. *Will Saturn do?*

One moment, he said. He clambered after her. *Wherever you go, I go. Perhaps, if it's nice, we'll stay.*

Play With Me

I've been digging up dolls all autumn. Headless porcelain bodies, or just an arm. Some as small as a quarter. I lay them in a line along the bedroom window before I sleep. Evening slaps their skin. Black air underneath the sill.

I dig and dig. Wet grit of the yard stains my nails. Mud becomes a dark glove. Leaves tangle my hair. It seems like I am always bent in the dirt, but this is not true.

Mother watches over me while I dream, while I dig. Mother's forever bed is beneath the rhododendron.

When I am not sleeping, and I am not digging, I creep out of the watchful gaze of always silent Mother. I stuff the doll parts in the deep pockets of my gingham dress and I go over the hill and below the bridge and I hum and sing and watch the dolls play in the stream. I love to hear them laugh.

Crow comes to sit by the bank. Crow never plays, but has lots of opinions on the rules. I say, *Listen here, Crow. You can't just sit there and criticize and nitpick.* But I don't really mean it, because Crow is a fine audience, and that's enough for me, really.

They call me alone. They call me orphan, the townspeople. As if I am a woman without. They do not know about all of my friends—Crow, the baby doll heads with rubbed-off eyes, Mother.

Every time the dolls drown, I put them back in the ground, and we start all over again.

The Things She Did

My mother killed her brother on my thirty-third birthday. The date has nothing to do with the crime. It's just how it happened. Late morning, I opened presents from my husband, Jay. I tied a red ribbon from the pile of wrappings in my hair. He handed me the phone. I listened for a bit as my father spoke. I said *Yes* and *I understand* and *Okay* and then I hung up. Jay watched me untie the ribbon. He watched me sit cross-legged in front of the lit hearth. I went deep down inside myself, back to that back corner of my being.

Honey, he said. *What was that about?*

But I didn't speak. I was gone. I was good at going. Doctors called it a disorder, but I called it a talent. An hour passed before I could talk, and I told Jay what my father had said, and we went to bed and didn't rise until dusk.

A mother's crime becomes her daughter's crime. The daughter takes the film of blood and the list of charges and drapes them like a shawl around her bare shoulders. Being an only child, I got it concentrated and pure. Something to make me feel more alive before it made me feel like I was on my way to meet Christ.

For a week I didn't say her name. The TV stayed off. The computer cold and blank in the downstairs office. I rearranged the furniture, put the dining table in the bedroom, moved the dresser into the kitchen, felt my heart hammer while I tried to sleep.

Then Jay turned the TV on. I divided into myself. He cooked each meal, coming home from the office during his lunch breaks. I only sucked salt off pretzel sticks, washed the plates. It was all I could do.

The things my mother did.

Ran her brother over in his driveway.

Had worked for a diner on Front Street in Poulsbo. Had braided my hair until I turned thirteen. Ate chocolate in her sleep. Backed up over his body. Sang me *Happy Birthday* each year in Spanish and French and German. Brought me books from the library when, as a girl, I would lie in bed sick. Once raised her hand to slap me, but then lowered it. Spent Saturdays working in the community garden. Volunteered to teach Sunday school. Wore Mickey Mouse t-shirts. And didn't talk about her brother for a year, then talked about her brother nonstop for five, said she loved him, said she feared him, said once he choked her, once kicked her, hit her too many times to count.

The piece she couldn't get, couldn't wrap her brain around, though, was on each attack he wore red. The cruelty she understood, in a way. It was their heritage. But when he came calling, a quick check of his clothes through the peephole told her if she should answer the door. At least it had in the past. Because now he was dead, and in some basement a detective peeled away a red button-down and bagged it for the trial.

I should have known better. I guess a part of me did. Maybe I wanted to prove to myself who she was. Her faces confused me. Monster and Saint. Saint and Monster.

I wore my red dress to visit her. A low-cut number with delicate beadwork like a cherry-stained wedding gown. It was cruel of me, but then I would have said I didn't do it on purpose. It was an accident. A fluke. Never mind the dress had never been worn. Never mind I took it off and on and off and on before I left the house that morning.

Jay said, *Are you sure?* He looked me over.

Sure of what? I said.

Well, he said, and nodded at my chest. I thought he meant my cleavage.

I put a red cardigan on and left.

Growing up, Dr. Dern asked me where I went when I dissociated. I had many rooms up there in my divided mind, but I didn't see how that was his business. He wanted to know what I was running from. I said I wasn't running and he said I was avoiding the question. I said it's not avoiding. I'm protecting myself, and he said, *Yes, you are a smart, smart girl.*

Smart girls don't tempt the devil. I was a bull's-eye, a bloody Rorschach blot, walking into the prison flaunting my muleta.

When I was ten, I watched a squirrel tease a stray cat. The critter fluffed its tail and ran circles around the bottom half of a tree, chirping like it had something to say. And the cat, ears back, pounced. *What a waste*, I had thought.

At Clallam Bay Corrections Center, a prison guard told me he hadn't believed my mother to really be dangerous. Which was why he wasn't paying attention when she lunged at me.

Was it her Southern accent? She's not from here, you know, I said to him years later when I saw him at the grocery store.

He rocked on his feet, holding a head of lettuce. *Yes, I think that was a chunk of it*, he said. *And her smile's a little lopsided.*

You're not the first, I said.

The scar's a nice one, right in the middle of my forehead. It wasn't her hands that made it, but the side of the table as she slammed my head down. Thing is, it looks like a consecration, like she had touched my forehead and given me eternal life. As if the table's edge bestowed an undying blessing. There was so much red.

I live in the forefront of my mind now. Bent over with blood running along my chest onto the tiled floor, I knew there was no crime worse than this blessing. Two men on her, holding back her arms before she could strike a second time. Everything from here on out is holy.

My Cat Called Chester

He kept coming to me with bite marks. I didn't know that's what they were at first. I just found them real curious. My stomach would flip when I'd see new ones.

Saturday the marks were distinct. At the top of Chester's spine where he couldn't reach.

I decided to keep him inside. He didn't like it. He kept knocking his water bowl over in protest, which annoyed me extra because the floors were wood and I rented.

Indoors he got bit, too. I carried him around, put him in a crate in the sink when I cooked, watched him out of the corner of my eye.

If I went to work, he sat curled up beneath the desk. My bosses Donnie and Dan said they didn't see any marks. I pointed, pulled back Chester's hair. Donnie looked closer, looked at me. He shook his head and walked off, but I made them good money so they kept zipped up about it.

Back home, more marks surfaced whenever I turned from Chester to take a shower. He hates water, which meant I couldn't bring him in. I switched to baths, minded him from over the rim.

That stopped it for a while. Until it happened in the early hours. I chewed pills to keep awake. Not sure of their name. They were blue and from the man in the alley. I just said, *Something so I don't sleep.* He never let me down.

When I was a little girl, my daddy always told me watch out for the devil. He's around just about as much as God is. He's even more subtle and glittery than God. I got to praying, figured it couldn't hurt, but it did hurt. Chester got bit more.

I wish I could say it ended. And a lot did end. Donnie and Dan's. My casual fling with the custodian. My landlord told me, arms crossed at his chest, that things were no longer a good fit and I best be going.

Some nights, watching through the trees into our old window, where the new tenant brushes her hair, I think I've been a fool. Then I think I've done real good. Chester and I are together. We have stars, muffins thrown out from Ma's Diner, a favorite log. Chester's still getting bit alright, but we're happy. I just say his name and he purrs.

The Club

The next-door neighbor Mrs. Green let us take what we wanted from the garage each time we visited. I chose a rusty spade. My brother grabbed a mason jar of marbles. I was a pack rat, even then, so the visits felt a bit sacred, like I was getting closer to complete. Not that I really could have explained that then. I was a child. But that's how it was.

With my spade, I dug into the hill behind the kitchen. I uncovered a worm, then felt sorry I'd disturbed it. I laid in the grass, waited for the sun to bleach my hair, had been doing so off and on for months. Still I had a head of brown.

I eventually gave up, went inside. I got out the phonebook, found where Mother had circled my best friend's home number. I dialed wrong the first time and got someone who sounded like they had a frog in their throat. Then I got it right and Laura's mother answered, said one moment, and Laura came on the line all out of breath and I invited her over, told her we could go to Mrs. Green's, get a little something for ourselves. I said I thought maybe Mrs. Green needed a friend, what with her wife gone. But really I just wanted the copper wire I'd seen earlier in a corner. Laura paused, then told me her mother said I was a bad influence and she wouldn't be visiting anymore. I hung up and cried. I wandered into the bathroom, looked at my brown hair in the mirror and punched the mirror, hurt my knuckles.

That's the same day my parents discovered my brother's cockatoo dead. Must have been from thirst, Mother supposed. I knew it wasn't my brother's fault. He was bigger than me, though not big enough to keep a thing alive without help.

I found him on that gentle hill with his jar of marbles. He was eating one after the other. Clouds had moved in, fat drops of rain hitting his head.

You're going to make Father mad. Stop that, I said.

I feel weird, he said.

Splotches of wet dotted my shirt.

You ever heard of a rain club? I said, sitting beside him.

He shook his head from side to side.

Well it's a club where you stay out in the rain and whoever gets the most wet wins.

Sounds stupid, he said.

Yeah, I said, put my hands in my lap. *Do you think I'm bad?* I asked him.

Course not, he said. *Do you think I'm a bad person?*

Course not, I said. *I'm sorry about your bird.*

Yeah, he said.

The rain kicked up. I glanced over at Mrs. Green's house, all the curtains pulled tight. After a bit of time her back door swung open and she stepped out. She didn't turn toward us. She just stood there, getting drenched. Minutes passed, her house gown soaked good, then she studied the sky, looked like she said something to nothing, went inside.

You want to bury the bird? I asked my brother.

Let's stay out here, he said.

I laid down, my hair in the mud. I watched the back of his head. He upturned the mason jar and the marbles descended the hill, then slowed in the wet grass.

You sure you don't want to go in? I asked. I felt cold. I wanted that wire.

A little longer, he said. *Just a little longer.*

The Sleeping Cure

A week before the cure, the yard's lone pear tree waved pregnant branches. Further off, the stand of fir and cedar groaned. Coyotes yipped. The kitchen smelled greasy, the room sweating with the oven's heat, and in the sink Faith had piled the pots, pans, wooden utensils, metal instruments dirtied after cobbling together the duck breast, bourbon-glazed carrots, mashed potatoes with gravy. The melted butter, the lemon zest, the charred bread, spinach salad and homemade ginger dressing. Red cherries with whipped cream. Sparkling water with freshly torn mint. To Luke it seemed to be a type of overcompensation. A staged plea for absolution. He found her efforts—the table set with pressed napkins, a lone lit candle—distressing.

Ticktock, ticktock—the kitchen clock mocked him. He tried, for the challenge of it, to smile, though his skin felt stretched. His fingers to his mouth, he felt his chin quiver. She leaned across the table to refill his glass. Her blouse hanging open, he saw her naked chest, dark nipples. He only felt heartache.

He penciled in a bit more on his notepad.

What are you working on? she asked.

The new procedure, he said. *You have to keep eating, Faith.*

The sound of his pencil on paper sounded obscene to him. He drew a long curve, then scribbled in the margins, cursed when the lead broke.

What is it? she said. *What is it that you are drawing?*

The new procedure, he said again. *The thing you asked of me.*

The cure? she asked.

Sure, he said.

Can you tell me more about it? she asked.

Luke did not answer.

Something's changed, she said.

He raised his head. *Look what you've asked of me*, he said, clutching his notepad. His chair screeched as he pushed away from the table. He walked out, leaving a plate of oil and bone. The rain had moved on.

At the end of Burnt Mountain Road, the barn sits beneath evergreens and fog, and within the barn, Luke prepares his wife's body for a heart transplant. She is peaceful in her sleep, her limbs stilled by paralytics. Her lips look dry and pale.

The skylight, the lamp—they give such frail light. Luke sterilizes his tools. He knows he will need to replace the lamp's bulb soon, perhaps by the end of the week. While he works, he hums a song about snow, though autumn has just begun. Outside a crow keeps changing its call, a rattling click, then a guttural cry. Luke straps on his headlamp. He has done many heart transplants in his medical career. His hands have cupped, perhaps, thousands of organs—discolored kidneys, empty uteruses, the lung that aches. He adores the intimacy of the cracked torso, his fingers touching what no one else will ever touch.

Scent of turpentine, forest musk, antiseptic—yet over that, the smell of the bear carcass swells, the blood—bold, metallic, sweet. Its eyes now stuck in a lazy stare. Luke's footsteps are soft on the cement floor. The sound of Faith's breathing echoes. The brash crow outside unnerves him, only a little, while wind whips the cedar branches, a gale rousing the forest. The inside of the shed is not sparse, but it is neat, somewhat hygienic, holding a locked wooden desk, short bookshelf, a twin bed, freezer, an oversized ice chest. And, of course, the operating table on which his wife sleeps, unconscious.

His insomnious wife. Ethereal, she had haunted their green halls. Sometimes in a nightgown, sometimes in one of his button-downs. Lately, she had worn nothing despite the autumn's bite. Skin prickled as an ash's bark. As he works, a slit of light flickers over the shed's newly hung curtains, opaque as stone.

He makes the incision. With the electrical saw he cuts her sternum. Thirty seconds. That's all it takes to break the bone. The retractor pulls her open, and the loosened blood around her heart pools. The steady beat like birdsong.

At the very edge of Luke's awareness, doubt hisses. His hand slips, clammy with sweat. A furred black body, rumpled in the corner like a gunny sack, reeks of brackish iron. Before now, Luke's wife had been another—twisted by sadness, irritable with both the sun and rain. Mostly, she'd been restless, her eyes two bruises rubbed onto a porcelain face. The lamp's light flickers, then goes out, leaving only Luke's headlamp casting long shadows. He places Faith's heart in a chipped blue bowl. He sews the bear's heart into her breast.

This hour, his fist inside her chest—they'd built toward the moment, steadily, since their marriage's beginning.

He had wed Faith in a white church beside a withered creek. The honeymoon had lasted too long. After Saint Lucia, they arrived at their house bronzed and sluggish, and Luke observed then, for the first time, his wife's seeming refusal to sleep. Before the wedding he hadn't noticed, perhaps because the sex and wine and her pale, soft knees had distracted him, as well as her fingers, how they seemed to always taste like fresh berries. He would nibble at her palms, back when it still felt natural to be playful, uninhibited, and she would laugh, pull away, pull near.

Their fourth week of marriage, retiring early in their honey-colored sheets, Faith nuzzled his neck. Outside the window—dusk.

Sing me a lullaby, she said to him. Like a child. She placed her hand on his chest.

What, he said, but not a question.

Sing to me.

You can't sleep?

I can't, she said.

He rolled over on his side, studied his wife nestled in his late mother's quilt, her eyes rimmed with gray. When she pressed her unclothed flesh against him, he stiffened with desire. She smelled like cut fruit. Luke cleared his throat, then hummed, monotone.

Sing, she said.

His song was a whisper. He could only think of hymns, those gory lyrics he mouthed along to each Sunday as a little boy. Faith snuggled close, her hot breath on his neck, her eyes wide open.

Here will I set up my rest, he sang. *My fluctuating heart. From the haven of his breast, shall never more depart.*

Faith's lashes trembled against his skin. A black bear came out of the forest. It padded through what would one day be the garden. In the future, she'd plant snap peas and heirloom tomatoes and even, quite unsuccessfully, an avocado tree. The bear circled the house, raised its body to peer inside the bedroom window. Luke sang, oblivious to the bear's round, yellow gaze.

Too bad you can't hibernate like a bear, he'd said once when he'd found her standing at a window, crying from fatigue and frustration. It was meant to be a joke to cut the tension. Her insomnia had turned critical. Her brain was not right. She'd told him she heard children inside the walls. Shadows wanted her. Her skin hurt all over. Once, she went for nine days wide-awake, or so she said. He could not watch over her ceaselessly, as if he were her keeper. He had given her numerous pills, prescribed hypnosis, sun therapy, religion. She was uncurable.

Down on her knees, she immediately fell.

Do it, she said.

Do what? He tried to pull her back up, to hold her, but she resisted him, stayed kneeled before him in a posture of prayer.

Make me hibernate, she said.

She was mad with exhaustion, he knew it.

How would you do it? she asked him. *Figure it out. Make me sleep.*

Faith, that's not possible, he said.

Do you love me? she asked.

Yes, he said.

Then figure it out, because I'm dying. You can see that, right?

He took her hands. *I can see that. I can*, he said. He kissed her palms.

Many nights afterwards he followed her around trying to talk her out of it. But one evening, he found her in the kitchen with a butcher knife, stabbing at the dark. Only then did he relent. The next morning, he told her the plan and how she would immediately need to gorge, binge, so that she could survive the hibernation.

I'm never hungry, she'd said.

I don't care, he said. *You have to eat like a bear.*

Locked in the shed, he knows she sleeps deeply, though she comes in and out of the nothingness at moments. Luke is always by her side, watching her. When her eyes open, he coaxes her lips apart with his thumb, makes her drink. Sometimes he brings something soup-like that's cold, thin. Her body is turning on her, growing more delicate and ghost-colored. She had gained the required weight before he cut her open. She'd eaten cakes and steak and salmon from the nearby river, and her belly had swelled as if pregnant. Now she withers. Coarse hair mats her armpits and legs.

He keeps her warm with the bear's hide, which he fleshed and salted. She stinks of yellowed grass, mud. Sometimes when he checks on Faith, and the hide shifts over her shrinking frame, he feels an unease that is wholly foreign to him. He imagines for his wife there is no time—no day, week, month. Snow comes, snow goes. She never sees it.

His little wife—she hibernates. He is curing her, has cured her. Her insomnia—a dead thing. Brilliant—the ingenious husband. What a triumph of love, to give her a heart that makes her overwinter, and in the spring, come to with her body rested and ready for their marital bed, their terrific coupledom. She'll feel beholden and exquisitely rested. He knows this. It is what she asked of him, he tells himself, and therefore, it is right and good and kind and pure.

The first night of spring, Luke traces the tender scar between her breasts, considers its ridges and incredible length. Her nightgown is loosely tied. It is the dark's hour. He leaves her still hibernating in the shed, sleeps fitfully in their bed. The heat is turned up. The radiator hums. Full moon outside the window. Ticktock, ticktock. He smells like sweat, tinny and damp.

Slowly lifting out of a black dream, Luke comes to, makes out a noise in the hallway. Something scrabbles, like a rat. Then a loud sigh, the sigh of his beloved, awake. The bedroom door opening to nothing, then he sees his wife crawling toward him, moon-eyed, tongue wagging, white spittle on her lips.

Faith, he says. *You're up.*

There's a low growl in her throat. A tremble snakes up from Luke's gut to his teeth. Her face looks altered, her eyes set closer together, glowing golden. All he can think is to sing to her, to bring her to her body, because he recognizes, mercilessly—through the lunar light that hangs on her pink face—that he has made a mistake.

Amazing grace. The words wrong and gummy and his voice shuddering. *How sweet the sound.*

She is ravenous. She is fully awake.

She will walk into the forest, her mouth red-stained.

Sloan

They are here, though we never see them. They have made the town a liar. I can't know for sure when it started, because it was all so subtle, until it wasn't. I am confident, though, it has not always been this way. Before, we cheated and drank and grew and receded like all good places. Decent, close-knit with healthy suspicion. Gossip and pie and the only graveyard across from the only bar. On the coast, a place few visit. Because it's cold and wet on the peninsula. Sloan, Washington.

We try to move forward. Community picnics. Church. Bingo. One casserole in front of the other.

How do you scare a man to death?

They have had so much time in our homes, our flora, our minds.

My name is Orca. I am thirty-five years old. I am a widow. My town is a shadow's playground.

Another one, the mailman says. He leans into my rusted Subaru, hands me the envelope. His van sits on the side of the road. *I'm sorry I can't trace them.*

Duke's forever been considerate, lingers at my driveway's end to catch me when one of the letters arrives.

I can wait while you open it, he says.

He can always wait. His route isn't long, and it's dotted with vacant homes. But he offers, and I say, *Yes, please*. Every time.

I tear it open, nicking the stamp, sighing. It's the same as the last one, and the one before that. And the one before that one. Empty. No return address. The postmarks inconsistent—Florida, California, Montana. My address typed. Nine sent in total.

Thanks, I say, and tap his knuckles with the envelope. His fingers look pale and young, though his face has aged in the past few years, eyebrows peppered with gray.

I'm sorry I can't do anything, honey, he says. He leans far enough in that I smell the beer on his breath. Some of us have started to do that—desperately reach for each other, stand together as close as we can.

Is it happening to anyone else? I ask.

Not yet.

The waters at Sloan's edge do not heal. They are whitecapped, salt-filled. But I love this strait, our ashen sky. And besides, the thin pockmarked Center Street that crawls from the coast into town, intersecting Highway 112 for a quick second, this street is my motherland. The block sits crammed with a gas station, bar, my shop, the post office, and a diner called Ma's. Just up Center Street, a couple miles, the coast turns into rainforest that's been sliced apart. Ron's Trailer Park. The volunteer fire station and community center. A few roads snake further out, one leading to the chip mill and First Baptist Church, another meandering to my home, a three-bedroom rambler at a dead end.

The Olympic Peninsula clutches Sloan, population 94. Too small for a school, the kids ride out on the same bus each morning. Sand, woodland, and—crowded against these hemlocks—the soft gradations of mountains. Tourists would smother us if it weren't for the weather. Our buildings' walls breed moss. The church lawn grows more mushrooms than flowers.

Minivans and RVs come by in the summer. Men open wide their wallets and throw dollars on our counters like the paper has caught fire. We don't have much to sell, but what we do, they want, because by the time they've rounded out of Forks and turned away from Clallam Bay, or come the other direction and quit Port Angeles, you'd think they were famished pioneers straight out of frontier times, ready to cut up our livestock, except we don't have any. No grazing fields for that.

I said it's my motherland, and I mean it. My mother died here giving birth to me, because the ambulance was slow and she couldn't reach my father out felling timber. The stained carpet has of course been ripped out, but sometimes I walk through the space where she laid last and I feel something like midwinter on my neck.

Why Aunt June told me the details, I don't know. My mother disliked her sister much—I gathered that from my father. It's a good thing Aunt June lives on the east coast. No one to keep retelling the story of my mother's murder by my body. Not a soul said they blamed me. Though, at ten, I chatted with my aunt on the phone because my father thought it would be good for me to be close to a woman in the family, and I hung up, sobbing ugly, unable to rise off the floor. The service that Sunday was on the seven deadly sins, and Pastor Rick always had a thing for blood and gristle. Greed's not all that sexy. Neither is sloth. But murder. My father looked at me sideways. Pastor Rick spat. I didn't cry because I had already gone dull inside. I stuffed my shame sufficiently deep enough that you'd need a chisel to get at it.

Emotions stay buried for only so long, though. Everyone knows this.

I married a man with a neck tattoo. Blair was kind and smelled like dark soil. The wedding took place in the backyard of our closest friends, Jack and Lisa. My father and my older brother Tristan were the only other guests. My father, slick with sweat, cracked jokes about all the noise the crows made from the high phone wire.

It's not caw and response, guys. He poked Tristan in the ribs.

I went overboard on flowers. Buttercups and cockscomb and poppies. Pleased with myself, I was the happiest bride—my dress discount and my nails painted a stark white.

After the ceremony we ate pigs in a blanket and drank Coors. Tristan toasted us, called Blair his brother, a man he's honored to know. Lisa kept crying, never wiped her eyes. Jack hugged the breath out of me, slapped Blair on the back.

The sun decided to set, and loose threads from Blair's suit showed in the flushed light. We couldn't stop kissing.

Get a room, my father said, his Solo cup raised.

I had first met Blair when he stumbled into my bookstore to avoid the gale winds. Back in 1988. He'd just moved to town and was walking from his rented trailer to get a Coke. The gusts kicked up and he slipped inside to catch his breath. I was sitting with my feet on the desk, shoeless. It had been quiet all day, and I had the heater cranked, an expensive indulgence. But it was my birthday. My hand hunted in a drawer for chocolate while the other held open a novel. I was a cliché. He told me later it was love at first sight. He moved in after a month.

Calling it a bookstore, that's a half-truth. I wanted only books, but there are few leisure moments in Sloan, and even less expendable cash. Castoff paperbacks don't make a sustainable business, even though I stock plenty of Harlequins. Whiskey and *Roseanne* reruns take care of the hollow hours people find. I brought in crab nets, and then I brought in reels, and now the cash drawer is fine, almost, and the place is called Books and Bait. I keep all the fishing stuff in the backroom.

I have my regulars. Randell, an old family friend, likes to stop by with his three grandchildren to show them the worms in a bucket outside. They always want to keep one as a pet, and Randell always insists on paying me a nickel, which—with a little magic trick—I make disappear behind my fingers to the children's delight.

I have the store only because of my father. Back in the day, my parents bought the building, and my mother ran a small grocery, though after she died, he leased the place to whoever was senseless enough to open a business in Sloan.

When I turned twenty, he said, *Damn it, you're old enough now. And I don't give a shit. Run it into the ground if you want. The building is yours. I'm not fixing the leak in the back, though.*

And when I turned thirty, he said, *Damn it, I don't want to live in this house anymore. I'm moving to Port Angeles. Better dining over there. It's yours. Microwave needs replacing.*

The home where his wife died. Where his children grew. The linoleum peeling and the paint stained with oily handprints. Tiny bedrooms, a little larger than cells. Many windows. White walls. Gray shutters.

Tristan won't accept anything from our father. His job at the chip mill is good, and he earned his swagger. It's the type of step that makes grown women stutter.

I sometimes wonder if I should do more with the shop, but once our father stopped by and looked around the crowded shelves, changed my mind.

Books and Bait, huh? he said. *You know this is weird, right? Your mom would have loved this. Would have thought this was the dream. Is it?*

Yes, I said.

They don't respect me much—the women living here. They know I didn't make my own way, that I'm a business woman but it's all from daddy's pocket. They raise their round children, sweep their leaf-ridden stoops and hardly lift an eye when my hatchback speeds past. I've also never mothered, which means they don't know what to make of me. There is no little Orca. They think I am defective, a failure. In truth, I am simply not a mother in the heart of me. I have no desire.

I've heard the women's whispers. Better this emptiness than a lie.

I have three photographs of my mother where she's pregnant with me. In each she's got a book in her hands. My favorite is the one where she holds a paperback copy of *The Princess Bride*. Her chestnut hair falls in her face, her features lighter than mine, looking delicate for a woman on the coast. Her mouth is slightly open, like she's reading out loud.

She didn't come from these waters. My father fell in love with her when he went to see a buddy in Connecticut. She was a friend of a friend, and his visit, which he had planned to be a week, turned into a month. He sent her letters and then he sent her a plane ticket.

She made even the worst tolerable, he once said me, wringing his hands.

My father told ghost stories when I was growing up—mostly to Tristan while they fed the fireplace—but I'd sit against the wall in the hallway and eavesdrop. I realize now they knew I listened in. I'd press my spine flat to the cold wallpaper and overhear romances of agitated spirits, angry dead spouses, lights that flicker when the wind is still.

Like clockwork, when my father finished his storytelling, Tristan walked around the corner and led me by my hand to my bedroom. He knew I got spooked too easily. He tightened my blinds so that no dark fell into the tiny room. If my closet door was cracked, he closed it.

What happens now in Sloan has nothing to do with ghosts. The eyes on me are physical. I can feel the pulse behind them, though I've never seen them. There's no chill. No warmth. No otherworldly amendment. Just the suffocating knowing that I am watched by a thing with flesh and want.

I would welcome a ghost at this point.

...

Grief has nothing to do with it, either. I know what a psychiatrist would say, and it's not true. It's been happening since Blair was alive.

Last year, spring brought weeds, lots, and I finally put on gloves. I dug up three ferns that had nestled between the roots of saplings. I replanted them in a small stone-lined bed in the front yard. I tossed dandelions onto the thick horsetail in the side yard.

Three ferns. That's how many I replanted. I'm not a woman prone to landscaping, though I love cut flowers. When Blair saw my work, he pinched my waist.

The next morning arrived and I came out of the garage in my hatchback. I turned to my work and noticed it—one innocuous fern too many. I threw the car in park.

I knew I planted three, knew it in my bones. I saw in my memory the steps I made through the trees.

Three.

It's not true, I told myself. *I planted four. I forgot. My mind is not good these days.*

So it became four. And Blair also decided that yes, four is what he remembered. And we slept a little less. And I drank a little more.

Then the apples. One Monday we left in the morning, him to the chip mill, me to the shop, and when we returned, Red Delicious apples sat in the bowl where Granny Smiths had been a few hours before. Blair noticed them first. Probably because he's the one who loved Granny Smiths—always asked for them on the grocery list with a *please* underlined beside it.

He'd arrived home a half hour after me, walked in and kissed the back of my neck, then sat at the kitchen table to untie his shoes. He paused, his fingers stretched midair toward his laces.

Where did the apples go? he asked.

What? I said.

The apples. I thought we had Granny Smiths. Did you eat all of them? he said.

Come again? I said, my face over a pot of red sauce.

We had Granny Smiths in the bowl. Did you get different apples?

I glanced over my shoulder, tried to mask my annoyance. *I didn't get apples. I've been at work. What are you talking about?* I saw the red mass in the bowl in front of him. *Is this a joke?* I asked.

What? No. I thought we had Granny Smiths. These are red apples.

No shit, Sherlock, I said. It sounded meaner than I intended. *I don't know. I thought they were Granny Smiths, too. I guess we're both wrong.*

These weren't red this morning.

I put down my wooden spoon. *Blair, what? You want to tell me our apples are now miraculously a different color?*

Did you lock the door this morning? he asked.

Seriously, you think someone snuck in and changed our apples? Maybe Lisa and Jack did it as a trick? he said, his voice small.

Yeah, they changed our apples. They don't have better things to do. Are you feeling okay? Did something happen at work?

Blair walked to the bedroom to change his clothes, not saying another word.

After dinner, when he finished the dishes and I wiped the counters, I threw the apples out. They made a loud thud as they hit the bottom of the trash, their perfect skins waxy and brilliant.

There is nowhere on our land that they—these outsiders, these shadows—have not been. I sit on the rough rocks by the flowerbed, staring at the fourth fern, time clicking away like I have gone and turned to stone myself.

Doesn't every man have a favorite story he likes to relate over and over again, whether it's to his children or the barkeep? My father's was the Goblins Gate, some gorge down the Elwha—a slinky river not too many miles east of us, its mouth hanging open, swallowing the strait.

When my father told the story—my body pressed against the hallway, listening in—he made the house dark, shined a flashlight beneath his chin. I would peek around the corner, his features exaggerated by the shadows the small bulb cast. Tristan sat in front of him cross-legged. Mostly, I watched the outlines the flashlight threw on the opposite wall.

My father's voice went deeper by a couple of notches. *It was a dark and stormy night*, he'd say.

Really, Dad? My brother would roll his eyes. Not that Tristan ever got up and left, though. He sat through till the end every time.

The story started with a guy named Charles, who gave Goblins Gate its name. Ventured with other men in the late 1800s into the forest, got spooked. Said the throat of the gorge was like a monster. The stones had tortured faces.

Bad enough for a little girl to hear her father say rocks are alive and suffering. Worse to hear him say he saw it, too, when he hiked there in the 50s. My father claimed once he discovered the faces, their eyes would not leave him. Their pupils pulsed in and out of the dark as Sitkas cast needles about.

He told this story so many times I can recite it drunk. Occasionally, he added details, how the two bridges built there have been undone by the devil, and how the surrounding hemlocks devour children. More often, he focused on the faces in the rock.

I do not see faces in rocks, or throats of monsters in the swirl of rivers. No, I see something pale move outside my window. A moment, and it disappears.

I walk through the home, considering items that might have been moved, books maybe upside down, a loose doorknob, but I cannot bring myself to blame them for anything inside our bedroom, at the risk Blair might have touched these belongings right before his death. The pencil on his bedside seems strange, angled so it's partially suspended over the side of the nightstand. He preferred a BIC pen. And this lightbulb in his reading lamp—was it always dim? I turn it on once and then never again.

I often think of when Blair proposed on Halloween, 1990. We stayed home to watch my favorite film. I put on a costume, a blue and gold dress, red shoes. Snow White. He was my prince in pajamas. I drizzled extra butter on the popcorn, laid my legs across his lap. No trick-or-treaters had been by. The home sits too far off the road. At night—even with a floodlight on and the trim painted white—the house looks nearly inaccessible, like a fissure in the driveway might consume any visitors.

The Princess Bride wrapped up, the credits playing.

I want to show you something, Blair said.

He grabbed my coat from the rack and led me outside to the back porch. I shivered against him, looking up at the silhouettes of trees. Blair flipped the outdoor switch and Christmas lights, hundreds, startled the dark, pulsing around all the trunks, through the leaves.

He kneeled on one knee, didn't even need to say the words. I kneeled beside him and took his face in my hands.

Blair's grave rests a few yards from my mother's. The dirt beneath his headstone reminds me of Mars, rust-colored and sandy. All the other plots have grown over with grass and dandelions, though I will let nothing flourish on his.

I decorate his resting place like I did our wedding—with a glut of flowers. Today I bring daisies bought in Clallam Bay, the closest grocery store. The hatchback's passenger side is littered with clear plastic wrappers which, over the weeks, have held roses, carnations, snapdragons. I am too tired to throw the wrappers out, and when the sunshine catches the plastic, the empty seat glows.

I'm sorry, I tell the dirt, or him. I know he listens.

A beetle lands on the back of my hand. I taste salt on my lips, though the strait is a few miles away. Cold wind slaps a hand over my mouth.

I should have paid more attention to you, I say. *You were right. Something was wrong. Something is wrong.*

I hear the crunch of gravel beneath tires—another arriving to visit their dead. I turn to see Pastor Rick behind the wheel of his crew cab.

I'll see you tomorrow, I say to Blair. Mud stains on my knees and dew in my hair.

...

The way Blair died doesn't make sense. He had taken that curve so many times. Sheriff found his baseball cap in the bushes. Debris from his truck hung from branches. They wouldn't let me see his body, until they did, and all I could do was stand there, rigid as a stake in the ground. They must have led me away, because at some point I was no longer there. I can't remember his body then, only the metal's shimmer, the smell of gasoline.

The ambulance turned its lights off.

I laid in bed for one week.

When I sit on the back deck, facing the flood of greenery, I can nearly feel Blair's hand on my shoulder. If it is dusk, I imagine his figure in the growing shadows, snaking through the brush, gathering shape, a reimagined man.

His body is woven into this land's every inch, this town. Sloan is a storm of him.

I prefer always to be alone with his grave.

There has been another fatality. This time at the mill. Randell, the town's favorite grandpa, was unloading the chip trailer into the hopper and fell in.

His death is like a fissure through the community. The grief and shock are palpable. People don't really buy it either, that it was an accident. He'd done that task for years. No one blames his daughter for pulling her kids from school for a week.

Randell was a rare breed, had even lent Blair and me money back when the car broke down. A second sort of father to me. As a child, I had called him *Papa*.

I cannot go to the funeral. I cannot bury another man, no matter how much I loved him.

My brother Tristan comes by with a string of salmon. We clean the scales off on the back deck. An eagle cries, but I can't see it.

Something's happening, Tristan says, chopping off a head.

What's that? I ask.

Something's not right, he says.

Tell me more.

I don't know, sis. I live by myself, but I don't feel like I'm by myself anymore.

I put my knife down. If I acknowledge what he's really saying, it will make it real. I fake a smile. *Did you meet someone?* I ask.

That's not what I mean. It's not important. How are you holding up?

I'm okay. It's a lie. Noises keep me awake at night, and I hear scratching at the windows at all hours. Once, a voice. I'm considering a gun, but I've never used one.

Have you talked to Dad lately? Tristan asks.

I drove over there yesterday, I say. *He seems real happy still. Maybe a little bored. But new people have moved into the apartment complex in the past months, and one of them is pretty.*

Good, good, he says. I can tell he's not listening.

We work in silence. Branches whine in the wind. Tristan rubs his hands together.

All done, he says. *I have to go. I'll just take this one.* He reaches for the smallest fillet, wraps it in newsprint, avoids eye contact. I watch him open and close his mouth like he's trying to speak. He pats his pockets, pulls out a broken match and a few coins.

Tristan, do you want to talk?

No, no. He turns to leave, eyes lowered.

Losing our mother was hard on Tristan. Aunt June told me so. He was in the house when she died. An EMT worker found him sitting blank-faced in a corner of his bedroom. No one knows what he saw, and Tristan's never spoken of it.

When I was five and he was nine, I walked by his door and saw him staring out the window.

Do you want to play? I said.

He didn't turn around.

Tristan, do you want to play?

He stood unmoving.

Tristan, Tristan, Tristan! I took off my bracelet and threw it at his head, but he didn't budge.

I remember, even though I was young, that unsettled feeling that ran up my arms, that slid across my nape. How I hesitated there, watching him, before I burst into tears and ran to find our father.

What's wrong, Orca? our father said, rocking me in his arms on the deck.

Tristan won't play with me, I sobbed. But that wasn't the whole truth. I didn't have the words for it, how I knew some piece of my brother was missing, that I had just witnessed a void that pulsed with its own blood, a being in itself.

I eat each breakfast alone—toast and juice, toast and juice. Get ready for work, no one hogging the sink. Some locals come into Books and Bait, but mostly it's hours of watching the post office across the way, where there's not a lot of action either. In the evening, I leave the TV on so I have voices to talk to.

I should live a life, but without Blair everything is muted. I circle his ghost like a moon. Often, I stand at the crash site. Interrogating. Unbelieving. Then I go empty.

Lisa calls it grief, but the word sounds meaningless. Five letters can't hold what this is, though I practice it in the mirror.

Grief, I tell my reflection.

No, this must be more. Perhaps, whatever it is, I am creating it out of mud and memory. I breathe life into it, and soon it will have its own eyes, tongue, if it doesn't already.

When Tristan and I were young, our father told us of woodland spirits—paralyzing, hypnotizing, triggering insanity. Sharp-nailed, skin-thirsty, screeching and snickering between the firs, leading kids and women away to be eaten.

Don't whistle in the woods, our father told Tristan.

Ever since, my brother lowers his voice once he's treading into even the thinnest forest. Decades of reverence and fear. He steps lightly, like a branch's snap might call them out. Or maybe he just respects flora, the cluttered silence, but I think it's that old tale.

Our father had said, *Don't go in the woods alone. If you hear laughing children, turn back around.*

Something's not right with Sloan's coast—algae in the strait, a subtle red, a mouthful for us all.

The state says it won't hurt us, but it may hurt the shellfish, sucking up their oxygen when the blooms decay. It means less crab this season—many men's daily meal and currency. The tension in the air reeks.

Christ is telling us to listen, listen to Him, Pastor Rick says.

I don't know why I'm at church. It's a type of boredom or self-punishment. The eight cramped pews feel cold despite the summer gusts outside. Rick rocks back and forth at the pulpit—its arms stained from years of his sweating hands.

We cannot know what He wants unless we become quiet enough within ourselves to listen.

I didn't bring cash for the tithing plate. I try to do the math in my head to figure out how Rick pays for anything. I cross my legs, but that makes my dress too short. I know this, because Tom Peterson peeks over at my lap. There is only his wife and four other families present, since most people have better things to do, or different things to do.

Do these poisoned waters mean end times? Is Christ coming? Or is He already here, within your heart? Do you carry Him wherever you go always?

Beyond the window, a blackbird chases an eagle.

Doubt is the enemy of Christ, Rick says. *When you have doubt, you are separated from His love. Do not doubt that this is the beginning of the end. What is in front of you is reality—good and bad. You must choose.*

It takes a lot not to laugh. I tune Rick out, watch the light through the windows play on the old hardwood. He's been isolated here far too long, I think, fixated on the *Book of Revelation*, mimicking radio preachers. I'm wondering how many of God's men are actually sexually frustrated thespians, when I look up and see Rick is staring at me.

Is that what you think, Orca?

My mouth is open. I don't understand the question.

Is that what you think, Tom? Is that what you think, Reba? He claps his hands together once. *No, we must stand together against sin.*

Someone coughs. Someone smells of yeast and musk.

An overcast Saturday, and Lisa and Jack stop by the shop. I usually don't see Jack. He's often away at work or out at the bar when I'm around. I think he's gained weight. He's always been a big man—but now his body seems softer, more vulnerable, and his lips are chapped. They bleed a little when he smiles.

Lisa runs her hands over the racks.

You have new inventory, she says.

I know. It's amazing, but I actually do sell those things. Last week I went to Port Angeles, hit up garage sales. One guy gave me a whole box of books for a dollar. Just wanted to get rid of them. Anyhow, where are you two headed?

We're going to take a drive down the coast, she says. *Get some fresh air. Maybe even make the whole loop and stop by Lake Quinault. They closed Mud Lake because of the algae blooms.*

Jack keeps his back to me. He reads the spines on the shelves, or pretends to. A former police officer, he still stands like one, feet apart, knees slightly bent. It's been five years since there was that incident with a missing child—the event that broke Jack, made him leave the force—but he's held onto the old mannerisms. Lisa once told me he calls her *ma'am* when he gets flustered.

Watching him, I marvel at how our men of Sloan have been broken, how each has a distinct disturbance. He turns and sees me staring at him, and I swear he blushes.

We should be leaving, he says.

Have fun you two, I say. He wraps his arms around me. He smells gamy.

Lisa holds up a true crime paperback. *May I borrow this?* she asks.

I hand her a bag. As they walk out the door, I note the small knot at Jack's lower back, the faint bulge of a firearm.

Tristan has his hand down the garbage disposal.

What in the hell did you put in here? he asks.

I shrug. *You want to eat?* I say. *I have leftovers from the barbecue.*

Oh, Jesus, Orca. The whole town got food poisoning from that.

It was Mrs. Ray's potato salad, not the cold cuts. And it definitely wasn't the whole town. We're not that type of place. You know that. Not everyone went.

He glances at the fridge. *Yeah, I'll take some,* he says.

We both move about in silence for a while, until he clears his throat, stands straight. *Are you happy here?* he asks.

Huh? I squint at him, put down the tiny mustard and mayo packets in my hand.

Orca, he says.

What?

This house is like a tomb.

I know what he's getting at. I haven't touched a thing since Blair's death. His jacket hangs on a peg in the hallway.

There's ghosts in here. I'll give you that, I say.

Do you want help, like, putting things away? he asks.

I don't know. I can't just lay him aside. I can't be that graceful about it.

No one said anything about grace.

I did, I say. *If Blair's here, I'm here.*

Tristan opens his mouth like he wants to protest, but then he nods.

It's nice how you honor his memory, he says.

No, it's not. It's a sickness. I knock my knuckles on the counter. *Okay, get out of my sink. Wash your hands. Eat your sandwich.*

Another weekend comes and I go to the Sunday service. Afterwards, I stop by Lisa's, and she's in the yard gathering weeds when I drive up. She looks fragile next to the spruces, with her hair gathered on her head like a turnip and mud dirtying her cheeks.

Where've you been? she asks, taking in my dress when I get out of the car and stretch.

Church, I say.

What the hell?

I don't know, I say.

What was Rick talking about?

Fire and brimstone.

She stands and drops the weeds, brushes her hands on her hips. *You want coffee?*

No, I just came by to say hi and see if you need anything. I'm going into Port Angeles to see my dad.

She doesn't answer, instead squints at the trees. I can't read her, and I can always read her.

Yeah, there's something you can pick up, she finally says.

What's that?

Can you get one of those security stakes for the yard? One that says 24-Hour Security? Jack's been ranting about something

outside. Something about operatives, agents. He's making me kind
of nervous. If we just had a sign maybe it would calm him down.
Are you getting security for the house?
No, no. I just want the sign. It'll make Jack feel better, I think.
They're like ten dollars. It's just his PTSD acting up again.
You sure? I ask.
Yeah, I'll pay you back.
No, I mean you're sure it's his PTSD?
I married the guy, right? she says. *We go through this about*
every couple of years. You know this. I've told you. And it comes
out a little different each time. Boogeymen. It's all boogeymen.

They were here last night, again.

I exhausted myself yesterday after work—laundry strung up
in the backyard's one small sun patch, deck swept, house dusted,
scrubbed. Almost asleep in the too-big bed, I heard what sounded
like a twig snapping, and then another. My body stiffened. My
breathing shallowed. I laid as still as possible, listening, waiting.
For hours I could not sleep, and I even prayed, felt clumsy doing
so. Just moved my lips in the dark, silently.

This morning, I walk the perimeter of the house, but nothing
looks changed. My four ferns move in the breeze while thrushes
hop about. Sunlight tries to make its way to the soil.

I pull ragwort from the flowerbed, put off driving to the shop.
I glance toward the road and see the mailman Duke, the white
blotch of his van. I stand in the middle of the drive, wave my hands,
and he waves back, starts walking my way. He carries nothing.

Morning, he says when he's halfway up the drive. I could move
toward him, but I feel stuck to the dirt.

Good morning, I say.

When he reaches me, he cocks his head. He considers the ground. *First off, I don't like to get involved with these things,* he says.

What's that? I ask.

Well, I delivered to Evaline already, he says.

Yeah?

Well, you know.

Know what? I say.

The mood that takes me, it's the same as in grade school when my teacher Miss Ruth told me to stand in the corner and think about what I'd done, but I would crouch there not knowing, chewing on a fingernail, feeling ashamed and stupid.

After a long pause, I say, *Duke, you have to help me out here. I don't know what you're talking about.*

So it wasn't you?

Wasn't me what?

That left your—you know what—on her porch?

My what?

Britches, he says.

I turn away, as if seeing through the house to the clothesline in the back.

You mean my underwear?

Yeah, he says.

She thinks I left mine there?

They've got Orca *written on the tag. They were hanging on the doorknob.*

What? No. I don't write my name in my underwear. I'm not ten. And I sure wouldn't leave them on some married man's door.

Look, I know it's been hard without Blair.

I hold up both my hands. *No, don't. Don't you dare.*

Orca, listen. I know it's been hard.

Duke, I swear to God, please don't.

He sighs. *No mail today*, he says, turns and walks back down the drive.

I watch him the whole way. If he only knew—my body is Blair's, will be only Blair's. My hands reach out sometimes as if he might materialize. Sexless—even my chest. I never wear necklaces, because I refuse to draw anyone's eyes near.

Lisa's left two voicemails by the time I gather myself and enter my home. I don't go around the back of the yard to check the laundry on the line.

You're not at the shop, she says, when I call her back.

I'm not well, I say.

I know what you mean.

You do?

What? No. Sorry, she says. *Things have just been off here.*

I don't respond. I'm peering out the window, considering a woodpecker.

Can I come over? she asks. *Did you get the sign?*

Yeah. And can you bring a pack of cigarettes?

You don't smoke.

I know, I say.

I'm not bringing you cigarettes. I'll be right over.

Three hours pass. She never shows.

I will always remember the time Tristan got mad and took our father's favorite baseball cap outside, poured the spare gasoline on it. He was twelve, had watched too much TV that summer. He sometimes flipped to the forbidden channels while no one was around—except me, spying.

Our father had made him promise to clean his room, and until he did, Tristan couldn't go out into the woods.

I remember our father yelling, *What in the hell son? What are you doing?*

Tristan stood with a matchbook in his hand. A soggy hat at his feet. Miles of vegetation behind him. The wind flared.

Father tackled him. It looked like violence, but it was love. I ran into the house crying.

The rest of that summer our father watched him out of the corner of his eye. Paid babysitters extra. I know this, because everyone talked about it. Tristan—the ticking time bomb. The costly threat. Little motherless boy, who smells like grease and chews pencils in half. Throws pebbles at the girls.

I feared him and longed to protect him and longed to be protected from him and by him.

When the weather is wild enough, I see a scrap of that old Tristan. It creeps over him like a second skin. I bless it, quietly, to myself. I bless it and I ask it, please, to leave.

Tristan shows at my door while I'm pacing, worried about Lisa, trying to reach her on the phone again.

Goddamn, sis. What's gotten into you? he asks, standing in the doorway, his arms full of firewood.

My face feels flushed. There's spilled coffee on my blouse.

Lisa said she'd be by, I say.

Yeah, so?

He passes me, sets the wood in the hallway. He's always bringing me things lately, leaves stuff out on the deck. It's mid-July, though. I have no need for heat.

It's been over three hours, I say.

She probably forgot. Isn't she planning a trip to Naples soon? Maybe she got caught up doing that.

Yeah, Naples, Idaho. That doesn't take much planning.

Can I just say something? he says.

What?

You worry too much. Not everyone is as thoughtful and punctual as you. Speaking of, why aren't you at work?

I had a shitty morning.

Yeah? he says.

Duke came by, I say.

And?

And something weird happened.

Yeah?

Someone stole my underwear off the line.

There's an expression of horror on Tristan's face, and then it twists into a smile, and then he leans over laughing.

I'm sorry, sis. I'm sorry. Someone stole your underwear?

It's not funny, Tristan.

It's not. You're right. He straightens his spine, wipes his forehead. *Tell me, did they run them up the flagpole? he asks,* starts laughing again, but there's an edge to it, and his eyes seem dull.

Damn it, Tristan, I say. I walk away from him into the kitchen. He follows, apologizing, still smiling.

Tell me what happened, he says.

Duke said they were on Evaline's porch.

Evaline Stick-in-the-Mud Peterson? How'd they get there?

I don't know, Tristan. Duke said my name was written on the tag.

You do that? Label them?

Of course not, I say. *Someone did it to mess with me. And Duke doesn't believe me.*

What if a dog grabbed them or something? Took them over there?

They were hanging on the door handle. My name was on them.

Tristan rests against the counter. He's still chuckling to himself. *Who do you think did it?* he asks.

I don't know. I should probably go and try to find Lisa. See if she's okay.

She's okay. Everything's okay.

The phone rings on the wall next to Tristan, but he doesn't budge.

When I answer, Evaline's voice, shrill and powerful, reverberates through the tiny speaker. She's calling me a filthy whore, and I fumble to turn the volume down. Tristan takes the phone from me, hangs it back on the wall.

You didn't do anything, sis.

Why'd you do that? Now she's going to be even more angry when I call her back. I bite my tongue so I don't cry.

You don't need to call her back.

She lives a mile down the road. I have to at least try to make this right.

Let her cool off. Give it a minute.

We sit beside each other in Windsor chairs—one of the presents our parents got for their wedding, passed on to me. The wood is worn smoother on the right arm than the left on both of them.

Not a very nice trick to play, I say.

No, definitely not. Someone doesn't like you. Or someone does. Maybe a little boy with a crush, Tristan says.

It's them. They used to be more subtle.

Who is they? Tristan asks.

I don't answer. He starts to stand like he's leaving. I clear my throat.

Can we talk about what's going on, Tristan? I ask.

What do you mean?

You know what I mean.

He does, because he gives me an inadequate smile. His hands curl into loose fists.

You need sleep, he says. *You've got those circles under your eyes.*

I'm serious. I need to talk about this.

There's nothing to talk about. And even if there was, which there isn't, what would we do about it?

I don't know. Call the police.

And say what? Your underwear was stolen from a clothesline? That somebody played a trick on you straight out of grade school? he says.

I know that you know what I'm talking about, I say. *You have to know. Tell me you know.*

Get some rest. I'll check up on you later, he says, gets up, gives me a peck on the forehead and walks out the door, moving faster than normal, like he just remembered an errand. Or heard the call of a siren coming around the bend.

Shadows cannot be caught. They play with us. They move through our homes, stealthy as cats. I drive by Lisa's place, but her car's not there. I go into Port Angeles and kiss my father's cheek, and he asks why I'm visiting two days in a row, though he doesn't push for an answer. I purchase four spotlights, return to Sloan and make the house a full moon's face. I use the garden hose to muddy my driveway, so if they come to visit, they'll leave marks. The windows are bright. I can't sleep, but it's a type of victory, and I'm proud of myself.

Jack's in the hospital, Lisa tells me over the phone the next day. *He shot at something.*

What did he shoot at? I ask.

The window.

The window? Why?

I don't know, Orca. He says he saw something.

What did he see?

I don't know, she says. *He keeps telling me he doesn't know what it was either. He's been keeping the gun beside him in his chair. Sits and drinks night after night. Gun loaded. I've asked him why and I asked him to put the thing away and he's refused. And when he saw whatever he saw, he shot at it.*

Did he hurt himself? I ask.

No, thank God. He's in the hospital because he was shouting. A lot. It was scaring me and it worried the neighbors enough that they called the police and they figured it might be good if someone—a professional—talked to him. That's why I never came by yesterday.

We're both silent for a moment. I feel an itch in my throat. I want to talk to her about this shadow with so much agency, how it is finding me at all hours, how I understand Jack, how I wish he had better aim.

Do you want company? I ask.

Thanks, but I really need to sleep.

I'll leave the sign on your doorstep.

I love you, Orca. A thing she never says.

...

Nothing. Now there is nothing—no noise at night, no feeling of being watched. I even try to create it, see if maybe I can conjure it up like a spirit. Like a baptism, this void. I feel pure. I sleep.

I avoid Evaline. She called one other time, shouting and cussing. I didn't try to defend myself, because that's what the guilty do. I drive the slow way home, a dirt road that rolls back into the woods and reconnects to the main drag after a mile. I've come to like it, the extra minutes in the dusky trees. Once I pulled over, stepped into the forest and sobbed. It felt good to get it out. No one came by but a robin, fat and lazy.

Duke's gotten over whatever suspicion he had of me at least, or maybe he knows Sloan's too small of a town to keep on this way. He lingers at the end of my drive now, not to hand me empty envelopes, but to tell jokes. His breath smells like mint, and his shirts appear ironed.

Jack's out of the hospital. Lisa's been by with blackberries from their yard.

I talk to Blair's side of the bed in the dark, and sometimes, I swear his pillow feels warm.

A hearse drives through town at noon.

I put the *Back in Five Minutes* sign on the door and walk across to the post office where Duke is filling his bag.

What's the hearse about? I ask him. *One just went by.*

Nobody I know, he says.

There aren't that many of us, I say.

No shit.

I just stand there, not sure of what to do with my hands.

Maybe I'll find out on the rest of my route, he says.

He will find out nothing. We both know this. We both know no one has died, but we can't say it, because it's senseless, that pitch-black beast, with its tinted windows, creeping along at the exact speed limit, making a full circle through Sloan, then leaving the same way it came.

The house smells like roses, but chemical, fake. All the rooms. The scent is irrational. I am irrational. I cannot find the source. I get on my hands and knees, breathe in the carpet. I take out the trash. I open windows, peek in the attic. I enter the attic. I crawl around in the attic. I close the windows and open them again.

An emergency meeting is called at the community center. Overnight fliers for a missing dog are stapled on poles throughout Sloan. *Lost Pit Bull Named Chomp. Please call if sighted. Do not approach. Chomp is an attack dog and only responds to his owner.*

Jack and Lisa sit beside me. She reaches over and pats my knee. *Good times, huh?*

Who the hell's dog is this? a woman yells as soon as the meeting begins.

We're all cramped together. People have even brought their kids. There's the stench of perspiration in the air. It's been an abnormally hot August—dry, cloudless.

I can't leave Sammy alone to play outside now.

I've never even seen this mutt in my life.

The phone number doesn't work.

Is this a sick joke?

Has anyone called the goddamn sheriff?

It's all noise and bodies shifting everywhere, but a consensus is reached. Those with guns will carry them, looking for Chomp. Lisa, Jack, and I linger while the crowd files out.

This is insane, Lisa says into my ear.

Jack hasn't spoken a word. I'm all the way home before I realize I haven't spoken either.

I'm getting a mountain lion, Tristan tells me. He's leaning out of his truck, idling in my driveway.

A what? I notice his rifle propped against the passenger seat. I can't help it—I put my hands on my hips.

I don't need one. I just need to get away from my house for a while.

Are you going alone? I ask. *You look tired. I'm sorry, but are you sure about this?*

Tristan nods. *Just a couple of days. I'll bring you some.*

I'm not eating mountain lion, I say. *Be safe.*

He nods again, pulls onto the road. There's a knot in my stomach. He's driving too fast.

They've severed the electricity, all of Sloan's. Four days now. Powerline is down, Sheriff says. A car crashed into a pole. We all know that's a lie. Duke's asked around and there's no one owning up to a crash. He's checked the driveways, the streets. Just about everyone's vehicle is accounted for.

Tristan has not yet come home.

Someone shot Ron's dog, thought it was Chomp.

I sit in the shadows each night, listening to the wind. At times I think it carries voices. I have a lantern and candles, but they're not enough to cut my home's darkest corners.

The sun comes up in the morning, and I leave the house. I feel like these walls, these windows, might turn on me. Swallow me. I wonder if this is how it feels right before you lose your mind.

I hear a knock at my door in the evening. When I answer, I discover Tristan—mud-covered, wild-eyed.

I found them, he says. *You were right.* He follows me inside.

Found who? I ask, lighting another candle.

Them. I found them in the woods.

For a moment I cannot breathe. I hold myself up with the wall. Tristan walks past me and sits at the table, candlelight accentuating his gaunt features.

They're four miles into the woods, he says.

Mountain lions? I ask, though I know what he means.

Gloves. A box of latex gloves. And an empty can of sardines. The ground around it was tamped down, like people had been camping.

Oh. I turn from him, disappointed, though I know I shouldn't be. *Someone's been camping in the woods.*

It's all National Park back there, I say. *Of course, people have been camping. Folks wander off trails. Kids go to drink. Plenty make homes in there. Remember that family they found in 1985, living off berries and squirrels? The Wilsons? It means nothing.*

Tristan shakes his head. *No, this is different. I know it. You were right,* he says.

Like a child, I want to cover my ears.

Something's wrong, I say. *I'll give you that. Something is messing with Sloan. But gloves in the woods mean nothing.*

He looks like I've slapped him. I realize how proud he has been, to find the bogeyman, and I've taken that from him, won't let him have this one thing. When did he last sleep?

I sit, take his hands in mine. He breaks. He weeps at my table, bent in two in our mother's old chair.

Let me protect you, he says.

Come see me, my father says over the phone.

Power's finally on, and I am sitting at my desk in the shop, counting and recounting the money, trying to figure out some riddle. My fingers shake.

I'll be right there, I say. I want out of the shop. Any excuse will do. When I hang up, it hits me what's off. There's more cash than there should be. I don't make mistakes like this.

A dutiful daughter, I'm on the road. I feel uneasy, then I realize. My father has never once asked me to come before. He's hinted, sure. Said things like, *It's been dead quiet here.* Or, *The neighbor's kids came to visit last week. Sure did cheer them up.* But he's never been direct.

The sun is in my eyes the whole way to Port Angeles. I want to turn around and go back, but nowhere is quite right.

My father's skin is flushed, his hair unwashed, his clothes wrinkled. He sits with me on the couch, shoves envelopes into my hands.

Your brother brought these, he says.

He gestures toward them. I open a fat padded manila envelope of cash and one gold ring.

My father clears his throat. *Your mother's ring, to give to whoever he marries.*

I open the other envelope, trembling, and it is insurance papers. I throw everything on the coffee table.

What is this? I ask. *When was he here?* I fight the urge to yell.

Just before I called you. He said he wanted me to have these. To pass what I could onto you. To call you and get you out of town.

And you let him? You let him leave?

I couldn't have stopped him, he says.

Bullshit.

Darling, Orca.

You could have told me this on the phone. You should have called the police. I reach for my purse. *Now he's going to—I don't know. I have to get back.*

My father rises, his palms held out as if in surrender. I can't even meet his eyes.

Why didn't you stop him, Dad?

He touches my chin, and his fingers are wet with tears.

He swore he wouldn't hurt himself. But whatever he's going to do, he's going to do. I can't stop him this time. He wanted to keep you safe, and so do I.

Something burns. I smell smoke. The sky is a lavender gray. The afternoon moon is swallowed by the plume's smart tongue.

Ash in the air. Fire eating all of Center Street. I can't even drive past the stop sign. Cars file out of a dense cloud toward the coast, not slowing. I hear a siren and then another. The shouts of men. A child crying.

I pull over on Center Street and watch Sloan burn, and I know.

My brother, the arsonist. My brother, a self-made God of blaze. Defeating the devil with his own element.

Here in the smoke stands Blair. The ash whirls into a silhouette of my mother. Everywhere is Tristan, moving out of the flames between trees, disappearing forever into the green.

Publication Acknowledgments

Thank you to the editors and journals that first published these stories.

Automata: "All Our Little Ones"
The Cabinet of Heed: "Gone, Ralph, Gone"
Chapter House: "Gekker"
Coppice Prize Anthology: "No Eyes for Them"
Cutleaf: "Into the Sun"
FlashFlood: "Play With Me"
Free State Review: "My Cat Called Chester"
Hobart: "The Things She Did"
Inverted Syntax: "The Bright"
miniskirt magazine: "Please Enjoy Going Where You Are Going"
Three Drops from a Cauldron: "My Medusa"

"Tastes Like Rat" won the *Landing Zone Magazine* Flash Fiction Contest.

"The Things She Did" was republished in Italian in *Edizioni Black Coffee*.

Personal Acknowledgments

Deep gratitude to the people and organizations that have helped make this book a reality. Thank you to George Singleton, my first fiction teacher, who gave me a foundation. Thank you to Denton Loving for your editorial feedback. Much gratitude to KMA Sullivan and the team at YesYes Books for your careful readings, assistance, and hard work. Thank you to my father who has always supported my writing with unwavering enthusiasm. Thank you to my beloved Charlie, who has held my hand in every one of my creative endeavors. Your encouragement means everything. Your love is nourishment.

Lauren Davis is the author of the short story collection *The Nothing*. She is also the author of the poetry books *Home Beneath the Church* and *When I Drowned*, and the chapbooks *Each Wild Thing's Consent*, *The Missing Ones*, and *Sivvy*. She holds an MFA from the Bennington College Writing Seminars. Her stories, essays, poetry, interviews, and reviews have appeared in numerous literary publications and anthologies including *Prairie Schooner*, *Spillway*, *Poet Lore*, *Ninth Letter*, and elsewhere. Davis lives with her husband on the Olympic Peninsula in a Victorian seaport community.

Also by YesYes Books

RECENT CHAPBOOK COLLECTIONS

Vinyl 45s

Exit Pastoral by Aidan Forster
Crown for the Girl Inside by Lisa Low
Phantasmagossip by Sara Mae
The Year of the Sheep by Stacy Parke
Scavenger by Jessica Lynn Suchon
Unmonstrous by John Allen Taylor
Preparing the Body by Norma Liliana Valdez

Blue Note Editions

Kissing Caskets by Mahogany L. Browne
One Above One Below: Positions & Lamentations
      by Gala Mukomolova
The Porch (As Sanctuary) by Jae Nichelle

www.ingramcontent.com/pod-product-compliance
Lightning Source LLC
Chambersburg PA
CBHW070311040726
47501CB00019B/2272